Praise for the D
series and *Advent*

‘This series of vampire parodies is one of the funniest I’ve ever read.’
wondrousreads.com

‘Fantastically witty and hugely entertaining, this fun and accessible diary will appeal to any fan of *Twilight* or Adrian Mole, teenage or otherwise ...’
Goodreads.com

‘*Twilight* meets *Diary of a Wimpy Kid* in this inventive parody of both.’
guardianbookshop.co.uk

‘This hilarious book will have you laughing your head off as you learn of the misfortune of Nigel Mullet.’
Fresh Direction

‘Teens who are fans of the *Twilight* saga will love this laugh-out-loud parody.’
Woman’s Way

‘A funny light-hearted read.’
Books 4 Teens

‘Just the sort of book to encourage reluctant readers to decide reading is really worthwhile ... hilarious.’
Parents in Touch

Diary of a Wimpy Vampire won the Manchester Fiction City Award and the Lincolnshire Young People’s Book Award, and was short-listed for the Northern Ireland Book Award, the Worcestershire Teen Book Award and the Hampshire Book Award.

Tim Collins is originally from Manchester and now lives in London. He is the author of over twenty books including the *Diary of a Wimpy Vampire*, *Dorkius Maximus*, *Cosmic Colin* and *Monstrous Maud* series. His books have been translated into over thirty languages and have won awards in the UK and Germany.

THE ADVENTURES OF A WIMPY SUPERHERO

THE ADVENTURES OF A WIMPY SUPERHERO

TIM COLLINS

Michael O'Mara Books Limited

First published in Great Britain in 2015 by
Michael O'Mara Books Limited
9 Lion Yard
Tremadoc Road
London SW4 7NQ

A CIP catalogue record for this book is available from the British Library.

Papers used by Michael O'Mara Books Limited are natural, recyclable products made from wood grown in sustainable forests. The manufacturing processes conform to the environmental regulations of the country of origin.

ISBN: 978-1-78243-438-2 in paperback print format
ISBN: 978-1-78243-440-5 in e-book format

1 3 5 7 9 10 8 6 4 2

Designed and typeset by Envy Design

Illustrations by Andrew Pinder

Printed and bound by CPI Group (UK) Ltd, Croydon, CR0 4YY

www.mombooks.com

ACKNOWLEDGEMENTS

Thanks to Louise Dixon, George Maudsley, Andrew Pinder, Jo Wyton and everyone at Michael O'Mara Books.

FRIDAY 1ST JANUARY

I've decided to become a superhero. I'm tired of reading comics and watching movies and imagining fighting crime. I want to get out there and actually do it.

All I need is a name and a costume. And some crime, obviously. I'm not sure how much there is around here. Someone dumped a broken washing machine by the underpass the other day. Could this have been the work of a supervillain?

If so, I fully intend to track them down. Because

there's a new hero in town, and no evildoers are safe.

Watch out, crime. I'm coming for you.

SATURDAY 2ND JANUARY

I've examined my comic collection and it seems that many of the best superheroes are based on animals. All I've got to do now is find one that hasn't been done.

~~Cats~~
~~Spiders~~
~~Rats~~
Hamsters

That's it. Brilliant! Hamsters haven't been done. I'll be Hamsterman. I just need to give myself all the powers of a hamster.

I could get a radioactive one to bite me. That's the sort of thing they do in the comics. But I expect radioactive hamsters are quite hard to get hold of. If I bought a normal one and microwaved it, would it go radioactive? Or would it just explode, like a sachet that wasn't perforated before you put it in?

Also, what powers do hamsters even have? They can store things in their cheeks, but how could that help with crime fighting? Maybe I could put weapons in mine.

SUNDAY 3RD JANUARY

Okay, forget hamsters. That was a non-starter. Looking back at my comic collection, I've noticed that the superheroes who aren't based on animals are often named after their most amazing skill.

So, what are my amazing skills? Let me look at my last school report ...

Apparently my strengths are attendance, punctuality and volunteering to help the lunchtime supervisors.

So I could be ...

Attendance Man. *Because crime never takes a day off.*

Or maybe ...

Captain Punctual. *Always on time to fight crime.*

Or perhaps ...

Lunch Lady Man. *Telling crime to stop running in the hallways and keep the noise down or he'll report it.*

Hmm. I can't help but feel these are lacking something. I must have a better skill I can base my identity around.

UPDATE

I think I need to develop a superpower first and think of a name and costume afterwards.

Super strength would be a good one. I could definitely stop criminals with that.

A lot of my favourite superheroes developed super strength by exposing themselves to radiation. So I just need to find a nuclear power plant, steal some radioactive waste, rub it on myself and wait for my biceps to bulge.

UPDATE

It turns out that radioactive waste is more likely to give you cancer than super strength. Glad I checked that.

I could achieve super strength by going to the gym every day. But it costs a lot of money and you have to sign up for a year. Plus, you have to eat extra food while you're putting muscle on, and that's not going to be cheap. And keeping my identity secret from my parents will be hard if I bulk up to superhuman size.

I think I'll develop super intelligence instead. By the time I update this diary tomorrow, I expect I'll be

using lots of long words and coming up with cunning plans to outsmart supervillains.

MONDAY 4TH JANUARY

Last night I tried to give myself super intelligence by reading the whole of an encyclopaedia. I got as far as 'Aardvark' before falling asleep. I think I might need to learn speed-reading first. But I can remember that aardvarks are nocturnal, native to Africa and have more bones in their nose than any other mammal, so I think I'm well on my way to super intelligence.

Maybe I should become Aardvarkman. The whole nocturnal thing would work well, but my mask might get caught in elevator doors. No, I can't afford to take that risk. Back to the drawing board.

It was easy for my favourite superhero Ratman to come up with his identity. His parents were shot by a gangster in New York, then he saw a rat scuttling past, then he vowed to rid the city of crime while dressed as one. Simple.

I'm not saying I want anything that horrible to happen to me, but it would be nice if fate suggested an identity, because it's really hard to sit down and think of one.

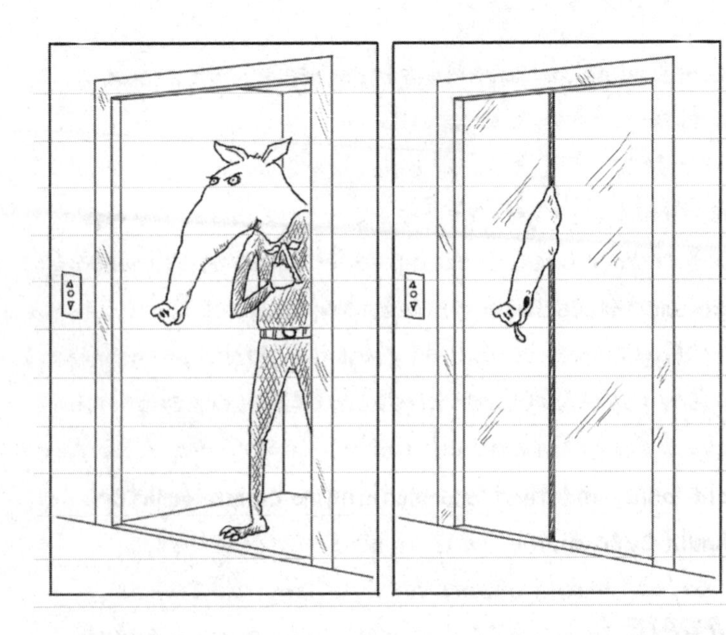

UPDATE

At school today I told my best friend Henry about my plan to become a superhero and he got overexcited as usual. He held his arms out, fastened his coat around his neck to make a cape and pretended to fly.

This is a serious attempt to battle crime, not a childish game. I hope I can get some more mature friends when I'm a superhero.

During history I tried to impress the girls from my class by talking about how I was going to become a hero. But they all got texts and had to look at their phones, which always happens when I try to talk to them.

I didn't mind, though. I shouldn't even have mentioned it. When you become a superhero, you have to turn your back on normal relationships. It's one of the sacrifices you make when you dedicate your life to fighting crime. If you get close to anyone, it only lets supervillains capture them and use them to lure you into a trap. You let your emotions take over from your cold logic, and that's something no crime-fighter should ever do.

UPDATE

Writing that last bit just gave me an amazing idea for an identity. I'll be The Loner. Pretty cool and mysterious, eh? Also, it lends itself to catchphrases like, 'You're never alone when The Loner's here' and

'Fighting crime is a lonely business, but someone has to do it.'

ANOTHER UPDATE

Okay, I have an identity. Now I need an origin story. All superheroes have origin stories.

I'm not the last of a race of superbeings exiled to Earth. Dad's company relocated when I was young, but that was from East Tadchester, not a dying planet full of superior beings.

I've never been experimented on by a secret government organization. I had a flu jab once, and I'm pretty sure the government were behind that, but it wasn't very secret. And it didn't turn my bones into a new type of metal and make claws shoot out of my hands with a cool 'SNIKT' noise.

And neither of my parents have been killed by gangsters. Our car got keyed outside McDonald's after Dad had an argument with a bald man about some barbeque sauce, so maybe I could avenge that.

It's not much, but I'll try and work it into an origin story.

Exiled from Tadchester at an early age, forced to watch his dad's car being vandalized and subjected to painful inoculations, Young Josh Walker dedicated his life to fighting crime. Whoever you are, whatever your problem, you can count on The Loner between 4 p.m. and 9.30 p.m. on weekdays and at any time on weekends and school holidays.

TUESDAY 5TH JANUARY

Terrible news. Henry has chosen to become my crime-fighting sidekick. I tried to explain I was called The Loner, which meant the whole sidekick thing wouldn't work, but he didn't listen. He's decided to call himself The Ninja Kid. He reckons there's a gap for a new martial arts-themed hero since the *Kaptain Karate* comic got cancelled.

There might be a gap, but there's no way Henry is the person to fill it. He doesn't know any martial arts, and has none of the coordination, strength or patience needed to learn them.

He's the only person in our class who's even worse than me at sports. He can't climb a rope or do the long jump without ending up flat on his face, so he's got no chance of taking out a supervillain with a ninja attack.

I'm going to put my foot down tomorrow and tell Henry he can't join me in the fight against evil.

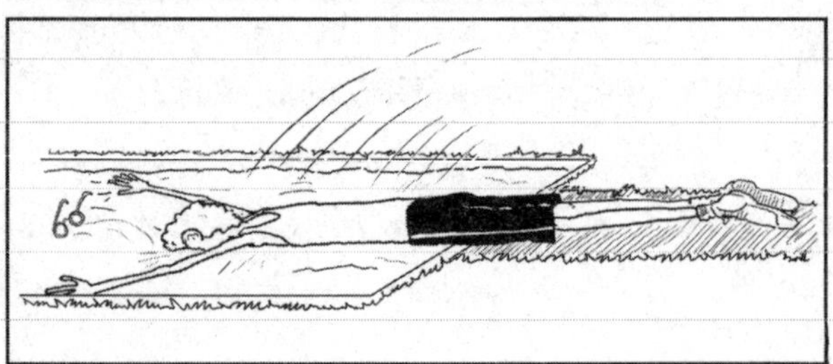

WEDNESDAY 6TH JANUARY

Henry brought his Ninja Kid costume into school today, and his mum had obviously put a lot of work into it, so I didn't have the heart to tell him he couldn't be my sidekick.

Why he got his mum involved at all, I have no idea. Now she knows his secret identity. All a supervillain would have to do would be to tie her to a chair, drench her in gasoline, light a match and she'd blab all his secrets. In fact, he wouldn't even have to bother with the gas, because she uses so much hairspray she's pretty flammable anyway.

Having said that, his disguise looks quite cool. It's made from bright orange Lycra with 'NK' initials on the front. It will strike fear into the hearts of criminals, and make it safer for Henry to cross roads at night.

At the risk of revealing my own secret identity, I've asked Henry's mum to make me a costume. I've designed a black Lycra body suit with a big yellow 'L' in the middle and a cape with 'Loner' written in yellow.

She's going to make it tonight. I can't wait.

THURSDAY 7TH JANUARY

What a disaster. Henry brought my superhero costume in today and it turns out his mum couldn't read my handwriting. Instead of sewing 'LONER' on the back, she's put 'LOSER'. And she used up all her yellow fabric so she can't even redo it. Typical.

She put a lot of work into it, so I suppose I'd better use it. And at least she made the fastenings out of Velcro, so I can easily take it off in an emergency. It might look cooler to have your cape attached to your mask like Ratman, but you won't look cool if it gets trapped in the engine of a jet.

Henry and I have told our parents we'll be at chess group after school tomorrow, but really we're going out to fight crime.

Watch out, supervillains. Because we're here

to kick butt and chew bubblegum. And we're all out of bubblegum.

FRIDAY 8TH JANUARY

After school we walked into the centre of town, through the shopping complex and over to the grocery store near the big crossroads, but we didn't see any crime.

It's much easier being a superhero if you live somewhere like New York. They have a lot of mobsters and criminal masterminds. All we saw were old people on motorized scooters, mothers with young kids and men in delivery vans.

I saw a man throw a cardboard coffee cup from a car window, which meant he was committing the crime of littering. Unfortunately, the cup bounced off a streetlight and went into a bin.

You may have won this time, mister car driver, but the net is closing in.

We were about to give up when I spotted it. Some genuine crime.

A man pulled into one of the disabled spaces at the front of the grocery store car park, got out, and walked straight inside. He didn't even have a limp or anything. There was no way he was really disabled, which meant he was using the space illegally.

It was time for us to spring into action.

We raced into the store and went to the nearest toilets to change into our disguises. There were only two stalls, and one of them was out of order. Henry went in first and took ages. I hoped the criminal was doing a big shop, because otherwise he'd have gone by the time we transformed.

When Henry was finally done, I dashed into the cubicle to pull my costume on. I could see why Henry took so long. There was only one dry patch on the floor, and it took ages to get into my costume without getting disgusting toilet-floor juice all over it.

We got outside just as the man was putting his shopping bags in the back of his car.

'Get out of that parking space,' I said. I put on a really deep and gravelly voice to scare the wrongdoer and protect my identity. 'You're not disabled!'

The man muttered something and continued loading his bags.

I wasn't sure what to do next. Unfortunately, Henry was.

'I am The Ninja Kid, this is my sidekick The Loser and we order you to stop!' he shouted.

'The Loner,' I said. 'I'm called The *Loner* and he's my sidekick, not the other way round.'

'You are breaking the law and must face our wrath!' shouted Henry.

He shoved the shopping cart into the man's groin, sending him crashing to the floor. The leg of his jeans rode up to to reveal a prosthetic limb. Oh God.

'Sorry,' I said. 'I'm so sorry.'

The man propped himself up on his elbows and stared at us.

'He didn't mean it!' I said. I picked up one of his shopping bags and lifted it into the back of his car. 'Let me help you with these.'

'There's two of them in fancy dress,' shouted a voice behind me. I turned to see a middle-aged woman in a grey tracksuit yelling into her phone. 'They're beating up a disabled man and stealing his shopping.'

As we ran back home I could hear a police siren approaching.

SATURDAY 9TH JANUARY

There was no mention of us in the papers this morning and nothing about us on television or online. That's good. We can just pretend yesterday didn't happen.

So what went wrong with our first crime-fighting mission? There were four mains areas:

1. We weren't very good at spotting crime.
2. We didn't have a plan for dealing with it when we did.
3. Henry pushed over a disabled man.

4. I forgot to use my catchphrase, 'You're never alone when The Loner's here.'

The last problem is easy to fix, and I've vowed never to bring Henry with me again, which takes care of the third. By assaulting an innocent member of the public, he caused more crime than he fought. So just by refusing to bring him again, I'm already doing my bit to stamp out crime.

The first two problems will need a bit more work:

1. I could go out later. Most serious crimes, like muggings and burglaries, happen after dark, so I'd be bound to spot plenty of evil. 'Criminals ply their cowardly trade under the cloak of darkness,' says Ratman in the *The Dark Rodent Rises*. 'That's why I live in the shadows.' I'll do the same, providing my parents agree to let me push my bedtime forward from half nine.

2. I could make a utility belt. Almost every other superhero has one and I can now see how dangerous it was to attempt to fight crime without one.

SUNDAY 10TH JANUARY

I've finished my belt now and it's looking good. I found my old Disneyland waist pack and tied a lot of useful stuff to it. I've got some plastic handcuffs, a torch, some scissors, some stink bombs and some bang snaps, which I can throw on the ground to make a loud noise.

These last two might not seem like important weapons, but they can create a vital distraction in the heat of battle. Theatricality and deception are just as important as brute force in the fight against crime, as any Ratman fan will tell you. He always lobs a couple of smoke bombs at villains before shooting them.

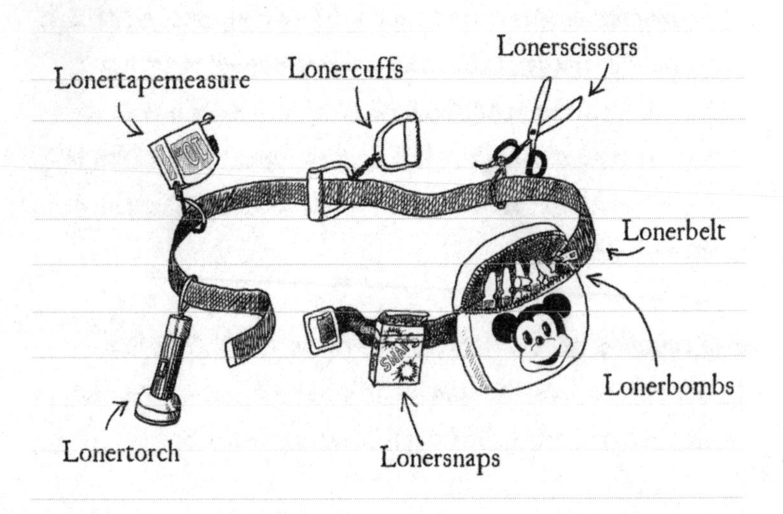

I also added a tape measure to my belt, though I'm not exactly sure why. I had space for it, so I thought I might as well bring it.

I'm coming for you, crime. And this time I'm bringing all hell with me.

MONDAY 11TH JANUARY

An abacus is a counting tool that was popular before the invention of calculators. They were made from beans on wires or stones in grooves on wood.

As you can see, I'm still working on my super intelligence. But it's hard to keep going through the boring encyclopaedia when I'm surrounded by my awesome comic collection. I have the second-best collection in the whole of our school, with a total of 452 comics, including every issue of *Ratman* and *Astonishingboy* printed since I could read. Only Henry has a better collection, because he gets more pocket money.

Whenever I'm reading my comics, I make sure my fingers only touch the white spaces at the edge of the pages so I don't smudge the ink. This means the comics stay in top condition, which is really important.

A mint copy of a really rare comic can sell for over a million dollars, so you should always preserve your collection. The most valuable comics are *Ratman* issue 1 from 1938, *Astonishingboy* issue 26 from 1943, which shows him giving Hitler a wedgie on the cover, and *Ratman* 368, from 1968, where the writer had a nervous breakdown and made him battle an evil giant trouser press. I don't own any of these but I reckon some of mine will be just as valuable by 2093.

I explain this to Dad every time he says I'm wasting money on comics. It's not a waste of money; it's an investment.

TUESDAY 12TH JANUARY

Today I got out of the Lonerbed, went to school using the Lonerbuspass, sat down at the Lonerdesk for a geography lesson and took out the Lonerpencilcase, Lonerpen, Lonerruler and Lonereraser.

Then I decided to stop naming everything after my identity, because it was getting annoying.

This evening I was looking through my collection of *Ratman* comics and I had a revelation. He doesn't have any superpowers! And yet he's an awesome hero. It just proves that you don't need powers to battle criminal masterminds.

It came as quite a relief, because I was getting really bored of trying to develop super intelligence. There's only so much information about abscesses you can take in.

I've never thought about it before, but Ratman just builds stuff like the Ratmobile, the Ratcopter and the Raterang, which mean he doesn't need a superpower. If a supervillian ever gets the better of him, he just retreats to the Ratcave and invents another brilliant bit of technology.

Obviously, Ratman has billions of dollars, which still gives him an advantage over me. I got £800 when my great aunt died, but most of that went on the Xbox.

If only there was a way I could amass a fortune, I could be just as heroic as Ratman... I've got it! All I need to do is buy a lottery ticket and win enough money to build an underground base and develop a ton of amazing stuff.

WEDNESDAY 13TH JANUARY

None of the places around here would sell me a scratch card, as they said I was too young. In the end I had to give some money to a man with a beard who smelled of vinegar to buy me some. He bought three and got himself a can of beer as commission.

I was really close to winning £50,000, but the last panel I scratched away revealed just £1. So it looks as though I'll have to put the underground weapons lab on hold.

Now I'm worried it might have been illegal for me to ask the odd-smelling man to buy the scratch cards. The problem with trying to fight crime is that you accidentally keep committing it.

THURSDAY 14TH JANUARY

One of the most important things about being a superhero is saying the right one-liners after you've defeated a supervillain. Crowds of bystanders will expect a top-quality zinger right away. Nothing is more awkward than keeping people waiting while you think of a pun. I need to prepare my one-liners now in case I'm too tired to think of them after battle.

So far I've come up with:

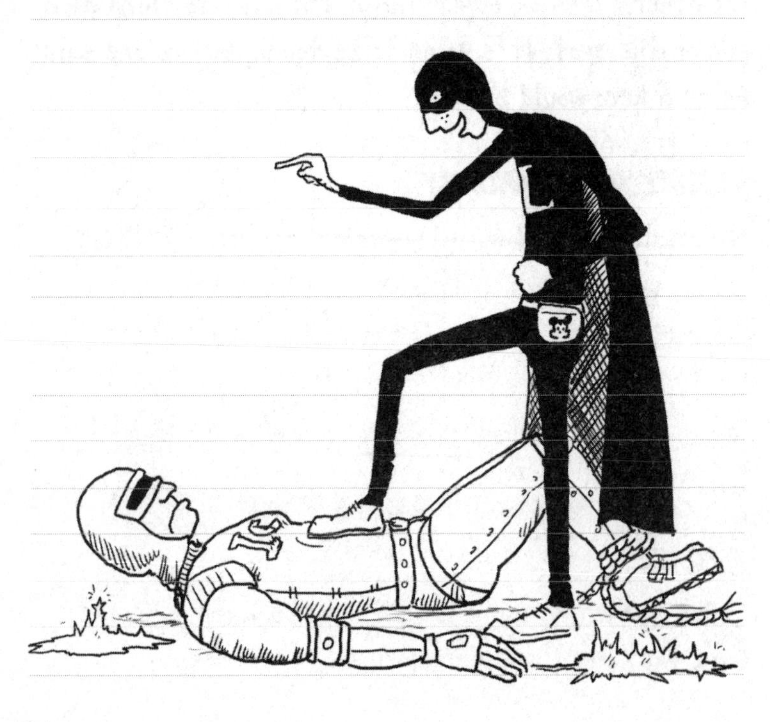

For when I've defeated a supervillain who uses ice:
Breaking the law is never cool.

For when I've defeated a supervillain who uses fire:
What's the matter? Am I too hot to handle?

For when I've defeated a cat-themed supervillainess:
Looks like you've had a major CATastrophe.

For other types of supervillain, I'll have to think of a pun on the spot. It's going to be tough, but no one said being a hero would be easy.

FRIDAY 15TH JANUARY

I've noticed that many superheroes work at their local newspaper as either a photographer or reporter. This gives them income to buy extra weapons and helps ensure good press coverage. I think I'll give the local paper a call and ask if I can work for them.

UPDATE

I just spoke to a woman at the newspaper, and she said they aren't hiring any new reporters or photographers at the moment. She said I can send her articles if I want, and she'll consider editing them and publishing them. I won't get any money for it, but it will look good to any future employers in the unlikely event my superhero career doesn't work out.

This doesn't solve my funding issues, but at least it will help me control my media coverage: supervillains won't be able to frame me for their crimes and turn the town's fickle masses against me. That's a massive problem for us heroes.

SATURDAY 16TH JANUARY

I went out to fight crime on my own today and I had much more success. I foiled three whole crimes, in fact. They weren't major ones, but it was a good start.

To save time, I patrolled the streets with my costume already on. A few people shouted at me and some boys in a car threw a bottle of Coke at me, but most people ignored me.

The first crime I spotted was a teenager dropping a hot dog wrapper on the ground. I ran over and asked him to put it in the bin, but he didn't hear me

because he had headphones in. In the end, I had to pick up the wrapper and put it in the bin myself.

Take that, crime!

Next I spotted a man plastering posters for a nightclub on the window of a derelict building. A quick check on my phone confirmed that this is called 'flyposting' and is illegal. When he was up his ladder, I kicked his paste over and ran away.

Another crime thwarted!

Finally, I saw a man with a beard sitting next to an ATM and asking people if they could spare any change.

SPLAT!
NAG!

Faster than a speeding bullet, I checked on my phone that begging was illegal and told him to stop.

Prepare to be wiped out, crime!

The man took a recorder out of his pocket and said he'd busk instead because that was legal. I checked on my phone and discovered he was telling the truth.

He then played a horrible tune that made everyone put their fingers in their ears. I felt guilty for forcing him to play the instrument and inflicting the horrible sound on everyone. But I still reduced crime and that's what counts.

I would have foiled more crimes but I started needing the toilet and wasn't sure what to do. Henry's mum didn't include a flap or zipper on my costume, and I'd have had to take the whole thing off if I wanted to go, which would have looked weird at a urinal.

I tried to ignore the urge, but it got too bad. I was glad Henry's mum had made me a black costume. At least no one would be able to see the dark patch if the worst happened.

I managed to make it home just in time to avoid disaster. It made me wonder what other superheroes do, because you never see them breaking off a fight with an arch-nemesis to strain their greens. Astonishingboy has superhuman endurance, so he can probably just hold it in. Steel Guy must have funnels built into his suit. And Ratman probably has some sort of flap on the back of his costume.

But it's Wolfmutant I feel sorry for. His fingernails turn into long, sharp claws every time he gets angry. He'd have to make sure he was totally calm before having a pee or the consequences would be dire.

SUNDAY 17TH JANUARY

I've written an article about my crime-fighting spree and I'm going to send it to the local paper under the pen name of Noel Hermit. I've even taken a selfie in

costume to go with it, so they won't need to send a photographer round.

I chose the name NOEL HERMIT because a hermit is someone who lives alone and separate from society like The Loner. And also because it's an anagram of I'M THE LONER and it's always good to give cryptic clues to your secret identity.

WHO IS THE MYSTERIOUS MASKED CRIME-FIGHTER?

BY NOEL HERMIT

A local crimewave has been thwarted by a totally amazing masked vigilante. Reports suggest that serious felonies such as begging, flyposting and littering have been halted by a dashing superhero known only as 'The Loner'. Local criminal gangs have so far declined to comment on the emergence of the masked crusader, although sources suggest they'll think twice about breaking the law in future.

shingboy
AB

UPDATE

Brilliant news! My article will be in Tuesday's edition of the paper! With the force of the media behind me, there'll be no stopping my crusade against crime now.

MONDAY 18TH JANUARY

I've been looking through my comics and I've had another fantastic idea. If I buy a military searchlight and stick a giant black 'L' on it, the police could shine it into the sky whenever they need my help.

My logo will be projected onto the clouds, and I'll be able to see it from my window. Lots of other people will see it too, so it will be great for public awareness.

UPDATE

I've just had a look at military searchlights online and they are far too expensive! Even if I saved all my birthday and Christmas money for ten years,

I'd never be able to afford one. But maybe the police will foot the bill, seeing as they're the ones who'll benefit.

ANOTHER UPDATE

I just called the police and they were really rude. The woman said I should stop wasting their time as people who've been robbed or attacked might need to get through. I tried to explain that it would help to prevent lots of crime if we worked side by side, but she hung up. Now I've given myself a sore throat from doing the Loner voice and it was all for nothing.

It's no wonder people like me have to take crime-fighting into their own hands when the official law enforcers are so unhelpful.

TUESDAY 19TH JANUARY

I rushed downstairs when I heard the local paper drop through our door this afternoon. I flipped it over to the front page. For some reason, there was an article about a new bus route in the town centre instead of my exclusive story.

I leafed through all the pages, but still couldn't

spot it. Finally, I saw it at the bottom of page fifteen. Not only had they given it a terrible placement, they'd completely changed it! I couldn't believe it! That's the last time I'm giving them a scoop.

LOCAL TEEN MAKES SUPER COSTUME FOR CHARITY

Noel Hermit has found a great way to raise money for charity – he's patrolling Dudchester in a superhero costume he made himself. Noel, 15, will be collecting for his school's charity appeal. Please give generously, as it's all for a super cause.

I don't know where she got all that nonsense about charity. I want justice, not spare change. Now I'll have people flinging money at me, which might even count as begging and make me a lawbreaker again.

Then the police will want to take my name, but I won't be able to give it to them without compromising my secret identity, and they'll put me in prison. And that's what I get for trusting the media.

WEDNESDAY 20TH JANUARY

I found Henry waiting for me outside school this morning with his hands on his hips.

'I saw that thing in the local paper,' he said. 'Why didn't you tell me you were doing charity stuff in costume?'

'I wasn't doing charity stuff,' I said.

'You weren't fighting crime without me, were you?' asked Henry.

'Of course not,' I said.

'Okay,' he said. 'Just make sure you text me if you're going out in costume. We agreed to be a crime-fighting duo, remember?'

I nodded, even though I don't remember making any official alliance with him. I let him come along the first time, and he totally messed things up. He failed to prove his worth as my sidekick, and I can't even have one anyway, because I'm called The Loner.

Henry held his arm out and ran into school shouting,

'Ninja Kid!', proving once again how unsuited he is to having a secret identity.

I don't know what to do now. I've told Henry I won't fight crime alone, and a true superhero must always keep his word. But I can't bring him because he'll mess everything up. And I can't stop fighting crime because there are innocent people who need saving. I've only been protecting this town for a few days and already I'm facing a dilemma. It's just like in the comics.

THURSDAY 21ST JANUARY

I took my mind off worrying about Henry today by designing some brilliant new superhero equipment.

The Lonercopter
Advantages: Handy for overhead pursuit of villains.
Disadvantages: Very expensive; town lacks helipads.

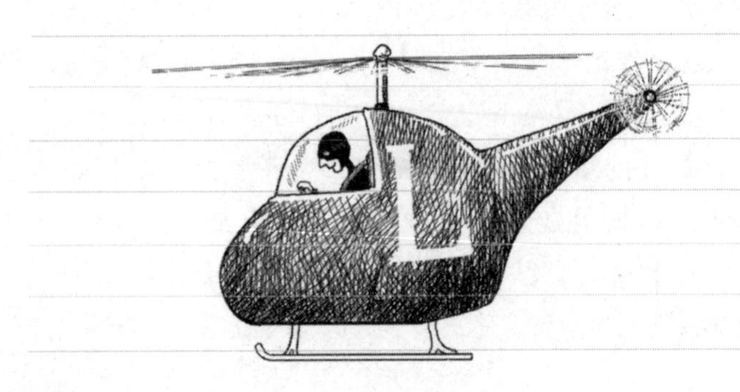

The Lonermobile

Advantages: Flameproof, bulletproof, 0-60 in two seconds.

Disadvantages: Traffic in town very bad; I can't drive.

The Lonercycle

Advantages: Good for the environment.

Disadvantages: Supervillains may have cars.

The Lonersub
Advantages: Undetectable to enemy radar.
Disadvantages: Most crime takes place out of water.

The Lonerbus
Advantages: Could be used to transport large numbers of innocent citizens back from enemy lair.
Disadvantages: Multi-seat vehicles don't sit well with Loner concept.

UPDATE

After considering all these options, I've decided to go for the Lonercycle. I already have a bike, so it was a no-brainer really.

FRIDAY 22ND JANUARY

I've resolved my dilemma. I'll go on another solo crime-fighting mission tonight, and just make sure Henry never finds out.

I'll pretend to go to bed at half nine as usual, but as soon as I hear Mum and Dad snoring, I'll change into my costume and jump from my bedroom window to the porch roof to the floor. By the time I've ridden the Lonercycle to the town centre, it will be after midnight, and I'll be into peak crime time.

Here goes!

UPDATE

I thought I might see some crime, but I wasn't expecting THAT.

I rode to the high street, tied my bike to a streetlight and started my patrol. Unfortunately, drunk people kept shouting at me, so I had to duck down one of the backstreets.

I felt quite mysterious and heroic as I flitted through the shadows. Like Ratman said, to conquer darkness you must become darkness.

I was wondering if I should scale one of the buildings when a van sped past. I was sure it was going over the

speed limit, so I ran after it to read the licence plate. I heard screeching brakes and wondered if they'd seen me and slowed down in fear. It turned out they were actually committing a massive crime.

The van slammed into the front of a department store and the huge glass doors shattered. Two men wearing black masks got out, ran inside and scooped

watches and bottles of perfume into bags as a shrill alarm rang.

There was no one else around. I was face to face with some serious crime and it was time to act. I told my body to rush forward and attack, but for some reason it didn't move.

Actually, that's not quite true. It trembled slightly.

Soon the men were back inside the van and speeding off. I managed to get a blurry photo of the vehicle as it passed, which was something. A few seconds later, I heard police sirens, so I ran back to my bike and went home. I know I should have stayed and given a description of the criminals to the police, but I didn't feel like talking to them after they were so rude the other day. I'm going to catch the criminals alone, and the glory will be all mine.

SATURDAY 23RD JANUARY

Today I uploaded the picture of the van to my computer and zoomed in. I spent ages making out the licence plate, but then I noticed it looked much cleaner than the rest of the van. This means the thieves must have taken the plates off a car and stuck them on their van. According to what I've read online, criminals do this quite often.

I've still got the photo to identify the van with. There's a dent in the left door, streaks of rust above the back wheels and a crack in the left wing mirror. All I need to do is patrol the streets until I spot the same van and then I can unleash some vigilante vengeance on the baddies.

Roaming the streets in search of a van might not sound very exciting, but detective work is an important part of superhero life. Proper comic fans will know that Ratman started out in *Amazing Detective Monthly* before he was given his own series. Even now, he's sometimes referred to as the 'world's greatest detective'.

His main method of investigation is dangling criminals off the edge of skyscrapers until they admit who they're working for. And it's always pretty

obvious anyway because the supervillains leave massive clues like playing cards. If he's the world's greatest detective, I'm pretty sure I can be in the top ten.

SUNDAY 24TH JANUARY

I spent ages patrolling the streets today but I

couldn't see any sign of the van. I found lots of beaten-up ones that looked similar, but when I checked my photo they didn't match.

I came back home to puzzle over the crime, but Mum was watching her DVD of *Les Misérables* with the volume really high and it was too distracting. I need somewhere to go and solve crimes in peace, so I'm going to convert our garage into a Lonercave. Mum and Dad only use it to store their gardening stuff, so they shouldn't disturb me too much – though I'll be really annoyed if I'm just about to piece a case together and Mum comes in hunting for her thorn-proof gloves.

UPDATE

I just carried my desk and laptop all the way into the garage before realizing the Wi-Fi doesn't reach that far. There's no point in having a superhero lair if you can't keep up with current events. There could be a massive attack on the town and I wouldn't know because I'd be stuck in there only thinking about crime, rather than trying to combat it.

When I got my stuff back inside, I looked into hiring a cave, but most of them are in rural areas without

much crime, so I'm not really sure why superheroes like them so much. I found a few plots of land that could be hired for gardening, but the Lonerplot doesn't sound as cool as the Lonercave.

Forget the Lonercave. I'll just have to solve crimes here in my bedroom with my fingers pressed in my ears so I can't hear 'I Dreamed a Dream'.

MONDAY 25TH JANUARY

I wore my costume underneath my school uniform today, so I'd be ready to avenge the criminals if I spotted them. Unfortunately, this made me really hot and by the time I got to school I was dripping with sweat.

I had two hours of physics this morning and the only free seat was right next to the radiator. I tried taking my jacket off, but my cape had bunched up into a weird shape under my shirt so I kept it on.

After just a few minutes everyone started teasing me about how much I stank. Mr Singh said I looked unwell and sent me to the school nurse, but I went home instead.

Superheroes must get quite stinky when you think about it. All that dried sweat, blood and mud would make their costumes reek, and planning your weekly wash must be a nightmare in a city where crime could strike at any time.

TUESDAY 26TH JANUARY

I'm really tired today because I got up early to secretly wash my costume. I don't usually wash my own clothes and it took me ages to work out the right setting. That's another bit of superhero life they don't show in the films – you never see a tense scene of a masked crime-fighter trying to work out if Lycra should go on the cottons or delicates setting.

I was so worried Mum might see my costume that I watched over the machine for the whole time. But by

the time the water had drained, she was on her way down for her coffee. I reached for my Lonersnaps and stink bombs to create a distraction, but realized I'd left my utility belt upstairs.

I flung the wet costume into a wash basket and tried to sneak past her, but she spotted it and sifted it out.

This was it. I'd have to reveal my secret identity to my parents and put them in great danger. Now it would just be a matter of time until they were bound and gagged in a warehouse and I'd have to choose between rescuing them and a busload of children.

'That's nice,' muttered Mum. 'Did you buy that with your birthday money?'

'Yes,' I said, and went upstairs.

I shouldn't have been surprised Mum didn't work out what's going on. She knows nothing about young people. For all she's aware, dressing up as a superhero could be the new hipster fashion.

WEDNESDAY 27TH JANUARY

We had to examine iodine solution on a petri dish in chemistry this afternoon, and we were only meant to use one drop, but I put lots on. I've noticed that some heroes accidentally give themselves superpowers by pushing the limits of science into dark and forbidden realms it wasn't meant to go, and I was trying to do the same. Unfortunately, I just ended up with brown goo all over my textbook.

I was clearing up the mess when I looked out of the window and spotted a white van pulling up at the traffic lights. I knew straight away it was the one I'd been searching for. It had the same dent and the same rust above the wheels.

I jumped up and dashed for the door. Mr Singh asked me what I was doing and I said I needed to be sick, which everyone seemed to think was hilarious. How typical of my ignorant classmates to mock me when they're the ones I'm risking my life to protect.

I made it out to the road just in time to see the van turning left. I ran after it, pushing my body to the limit in the pursuit of justice. After a few hundred metres I got an awful stitch and had to bend over and get my breath back. I knew I should have honed my superfitness.

Once my vision had stopped swimming, I spotted the van parked outside a hardware store. A bald man walked out of the store, got in the van and drove off. I tried to force myself to run after him, but the stitch came back. The number 17 bus pulled up next to me, so I thought I might as well get it in case the criminals were going the same way.

The driver made me lift my mask before accepting my pass, and insisted on pulling up at every stop, even if no one was getting on or off. I asked him to speed up because I was pursuing criminals, and he thought that was hilarious. Again, I was mocked by the very citizens I'm trying to help – no wonder other superheroes have to shell out for private transport such as the Ratmobile. If bus drivers would take us a little more seriously, we might be able to use public transport and save the planet as well as the lives of innocent townsfolk.

The last I saw of the white van, it was turning under the railway bridge into the Raven's Green area, so at least I know where to continue my search. I'm

heading straight down there after school tomorrow to dish out some justice.

THURSDAY 28TH JANUARY

I went back to where I saw the white van this evening. It's quite a rough area and I started getting nervous as it went dark. I kept imagining someone was going to try and rob my phone. But then I remembered I'm a crime-fighter and that's exactly the sort of thing I should want to happen now.

There were quite a few white vans in Raven's Green and I had to examine them all, which made people

twitch their curtains and stare at me. Foolish citizens! I was there to fight crime, not to steal hubcaps.

I finally spotted the van in the driveway of a house with an overgrown garden containing a couch and a mattress. Paint was flaking off the window frames and the drains were wonky. They clearly hadn't spent the proceeds of the robbery on home improvement.

So this was it. I'd found my enemies. Now it was time to change into my costume and open up a can of whoopass.

The curtain shuffled open and I saw the bald-headed man glaring out at me. I thought he looked like he'd be quite good at fighting. Then I remembered a really important fact. I'm not very good at it.

I beat Henry in a fight once, but I did that mostly

through tickling, and I doubted I'd be able to use the same tactic here.

On reflection, I decided it would be better to leave the whoopass in the can and run home.

Now I feel really ashamed. Maybe I should change my name to Captain Coward and admit that my special powers are running away, hiding and quaking.

FRIDAY 29TH JANUARY

I'm feeling better now because I've realized I can still prevent crime without resorting to violence. All I need to do is stake out the villains, wait until they commit another crime, film it on my phone and send it to the police.

I suppose technically that makes me a snitch rather than a hero, but I'll still have a costume and I'll still be combating crime, and that's good enough for me.

And there are lots of worse superheroes, anyway. There was Skate Girl, for example. She lasted just three issues back in 1983. She had a pair of roller skates built into her costume. If any of her foes went up stairs she'd have to search for an elevator or go home.

Then there was The Hearing Aid, who had supersensitive ears and lived in the middle of New York. His catchphrase was 'Please kill me'.

Worst of all was Time Warp, a superhero who could travel back in time, but only by three minutes. Whenever he turned up to fight a villain, he'd be greeted by a future version of himself telling him what he'd just done wrong. It made the whole comic a real downer.

Compared to that lot, I'll still be a decent hero.

SATURDAY 30TH JANUARY

Woah. That was a weird day.

This morning I told my parents I was going to a comic convention, when instead I went to stake out the criminal's house. I wore my costume, but put my big winter jacket over the top so I wouldn't attract attention.

I sat on a bench opposite the house and wondered if I'd turned up too early. Criminals do most of their misdeeds at night, so they probably spend most of the day asleep.

I played on my phone until the battery ran out and then stared at the dark house. Being a superhero involves much more waiting than you'd expect. It's just as well they leave those bits out of the comics.

It started drizzling in the afternoon and I was about to give up and go home when something dramatic actually happened. The bald man stepped out, got in the van and drove off. I was convinced he was off to commit another robbery, so I chased after him. I tried to shout, 'Fighting crime is a lonely business, but someone has to do it,' but it was too difficult while running. I should probably come up with a shorter catchphrase like 'shazam' or 'excelsior'.

I was focusing so much on the robber's van I didn't pay any attention to the black one that pulled up just ahead of me. As I drew level with it, the back doors opened and a man wearing an army uniform and a balaclava reached out and scooped me up by my underarms. He hurled me onto

the metal floor inside his van, knocking the wind out of me.

I was too shocked to understand what was going on. One second my feet were pounding the ground, the next I was lying on a cold floor between two wooden benches.

The man threw a cloth sack over my head and tied it tight around my waist with rope. I heard him clamber into the front seat and the van sped away.

How stupid of me – I should have guessed the criminals wouldn't be acting alone. Of course they'd have guards.

I tried to make my mouth say, 'Tell your friends to cease their robberies or you'll get a taste of justice'. But it said, 'Please don't kill me. I promise I won't tell anyone about the robberies.'

Trying to forget my brief lull in heroism, I managed to wrestle one of my hands under the rope and grabbed my utility belt. I unhooked one of the Lonersnaps and threw it against the side of the van. I was hoping the noise might startle the guard and make him crash, but you couldn't really hear it over the engine.

I tried throwing one of my stink bombs, but it

didn't have much effect either. The van was already quite smelly.

Finally, I found my Lonerscissors, unhooked them from their loop, lifted them to the rope and tried to snip it. Then I remembered I'd used them to cut thick cardboard when I was making my Ratman diorama last year. They couldn't even get through weak string now, never mind tough rope.

It was no use. I'd have to rely on my combat skills to get me out of the crisis.

The van pulled to a halt and I heard the doors open.

'Help!' I shouted. 'Kidnap!'

The man untied the rope and pulled off the sack. We were inside a spacious garage with bare breeze block walls. The man opened a door and beckoned me through.

'Please let me go,' I said. 'I won't tell anyone about your crimes.'

'I don't commit crimes,' he said. 'I fight them. And I think you do too. That's why I want to talk to you.'

I noticed the man's camouflage jacket had the words 'Army Dan' sewn on it.

'Are you a superhero too?' I asked.

'Don't be silly,' he said. 'Superheroes are for movies and comic books. I'm a costumed vigilante.'

It sounded good enough to me. I clambered out of the van and followed him through the door.

I emerged in a dark room surrounded by red and green flickering dots. Spotlights blinked on to reveal three leather couches in the middle of the room and three long metal desks covered in laptops, hard drives and monitors running along the walls.

The man nodded at one of the seats and I sat down.

'So you're The Loser, are you?' he asked, perching

on the arm of the opposite couch. 'Why do you want to fight crime?'

'The Loner,' I said. 'It was a spelling mistake. And I want to fight crime because I think it's wrong.'

'It's worse than wrong,' he said. 'It's evil. It's pernicious. It's a cancer.'

He whipped off his balaclava to reveal his red, scowling face. The veins on his temple were bulging and his eyes were wide.

'I think that too,' I said. I tried to work myself up to be as angry as him. 'I think crime is as bad as smudging a page of a limited edition comic because you read it too soon after eating chocolate. I think it's as bad as borrowing someone's Steel Guy action figure and returning it without the accessories. I think it's as bad as the 1960s *Ratman* TV series which failed to respect the source material.'

'I'm Army Dan,' he said. 'I'm fighting a war against criminals because the government are too soft to do anything about them.' He pressed his fingers to his temples and rubbed them. 'The streets are my battleground and knowledge is my weapon. As well as actual weapons. What about you?'

'I'm The Loner,' I said. 'And I work by myself.

Fighting crime is a lonely job, but someone's got to do it, that's what I always say.'

'So you wouldn't be interested in joining our costumed vigilante league, then?' he asked.

'On the other hand, I don't have to work by myself,' I said. 'Fighting crime doesn't have to be a lonely job, that's what I always say.'

SUNDAY 31ST JANUARY

It took me ages to convince Dan I hated crime as much as him. He asked me lots of questions about what sort of punishments criminals should get. I started off with sensible ones like community service and fines, but he wasn't impressed. It was only when I said that anyone who ever broke the law should be given the electric chair that he looked satisfied.

I hope he doesn't find out about the time Henry and I attacked that man with the false leg. We'd both have to be publicly executed under this new system.

'I can see you hate crime just as much as I do,' he said, slapping his hand on my shoulder. 'And there are others in this town who feel the same. But we can't have costumed vigilantes running around willy-nilly in broad daylight. The only way we can defeat crime is to join forces. Criminals have got discipline and co-ordination and we need it too.'

Dan said thinking about crime had made him so angry that he had to go to use his personal gym, so I had to leave. But I'm going back on Tuesday to attend my first meeting of The East Dudchester League of Costumed Vigilantes (incorporating The Central Region Masked Crime-Fighters Society). It's not a very catchy name, but Dan says it took them ages to agree on it, so I didn't criticize it.

Dan has been staking out the robbers for weeks now and reckons they're planning another big raid next weekend. He stopped me from running after them because he doesn't want them to know anyone's onto them. Now I see what he means about joining forces. On my own, I would only have recorded them committing a crime and passed my evidence on to the police. But now I'm in a team, I can hand out some proper vigilante justice.

Will it be pretty? Probably not. But they should have thought about that before they broke the law.

We're going to unleash the combined fury of The East Dudchester League of Costumed Vigilantes (incorporating The Central Region Masked Crime-

Fighters Society) and the baddies won't know what's hit them.

I still can't believe I've been invited to join a proper crime-fighting team. I haven't been this excited since I watched the live webcast of the *Ratman vs Astonishingboy* movie announcement at last year's ComicBinge Convention.

MONDAY 1ST FEBRUARY

We had a science quiz this morning, and I totally forgot about it. I got just five out of twenty, which was my worst ever score. I don't care, though. I've been invited to join a league of costumed vigilantes. That's the only qualification I'll need for an amazing future.

Henry came top of the class with nineteen out of twenty and tried to gloat at me in the lunch hall, but he could tell he was having no effect.

'Why have you stopped caring about tests?' he asked as he took his sandwiches out of his lunch box. 'Have you been fighting crime without me like you promised you wouldn't?'

'No,' I said. 'I found a mint copy of *Ratman* issue 36 in a charity shop for 30p and it made me too excited to revise.'

'Oh really?' asked Henry. 'Which cover does that one have again?'

Why did I try and lie about comics to Henry? I should have picked a topic he knows nothing about like sport or dancing or girls.

'It shows Ratman swinging on a rope with a skyscraper in the background,' I said.

'Nice try,' said Henry. 'But that only describes issues 3, 14, 15 and 92 from the golden age. That proves you've been fighting crime.'

I tried to eat my sandwich, but he kept prodding me in the cheek and asking me to tell him the truth. Of all the trials I thought I'd face as a costumed vigilante, I didn't expect being poked in the cheek while trying to eat a cheese and ham sandwich would feature highly. But I managed it, and I'm counting it as another heroic victory.

Henry can irritate me all he likes. I'm not getting him involved in the League. Our work is too important to let liabilities like him hang around.

TUESDAY 2ND FEBRUARY

I'm just back from my first meeting of The East Dudchester League of Costumed Vigilantes

(incorporating The Central Region Masked Crime-Fighters Society) and I'm too excited to sleep.

I arrived at Dan's house at half seven and he led me down a corridor with framed newspaper articles on the walls and large bottles of water stacked on the floor. He stopped in front of a bookshelf and pulled out a copy of *Crime and Punishment*. The shelf swung open like a door, revealing steps down to the basement I saw the other day. The other costumed vigilantes were waiting down there.

There was a middle-aged couple sitting on the sofa nearest to the garage door. A teenage girl was standing behind them and looking at her phone. They were all wearing green costumes with red capes and a blue letter 'A' sewn on the front.

'I'm Mr Amazing,' said the man. He put his arm around the woman. 'And this is my wife Mrs Amazing. And that's our daughter, Amazagirl.'

'Amy Gibson,' muttered the girl without taking her eyes off her phone.

'We agreed not to give away our real names, didn't we, dear?' asked Mr Amazing, forcing a smile.

'Whoops,' said Amazagirl. 'Silly me.'

There were two men over at the table by the far

wall. The first was holding a tangle of wires and the second was holding a circuit board.

'I'm Doctor Infinity,' said the first. He was wearing a blue costume with a sideways number eight on the front. 'And my desire to fight crime knows no limits.'

'And I'm Pi,' said the other. He was wearing a red costume with a funny squiggle on the front. 'And I'm irrational about crime.'

'I am a real doctor,' said Doctor Infinity. 'But only

of applied mathematics. So don't ask me for help with your medical ailments.'

'Unless you're suffering from a partial fraction,' said Pi.

They started laughing and I did my best to join in.

'I'm The Loner,' I said. I tried to say it in my secret deep voice, but it sent me into a coughing fit and everyone had to wait for it to stop.

Amazagirl looked up from her phone. 'You know it says "The Loser" on the back of your cape, right?'

'Printing error,' I said. 'But printing errors aren't important. Fighting crime is. And I hate crime.'

'Good,' said Army Dan. 'Because we all hate crime too, don't we?'

'Yes,' said Mr Amazing.

'Absolutely,' said Mrs Amazing.

'Affirmative,' said Doctor Infinity and Pi.

'Technically vigilantism is illegal too,' said Amazagirl. 'So that means we hate ourselves. Which is understandable.'

Dan wandered over to one of the tables and picked up a black box with four aerials. 'We've been intercepting the gang's phone calls and we've discovered they're planning to ram raid an electronics

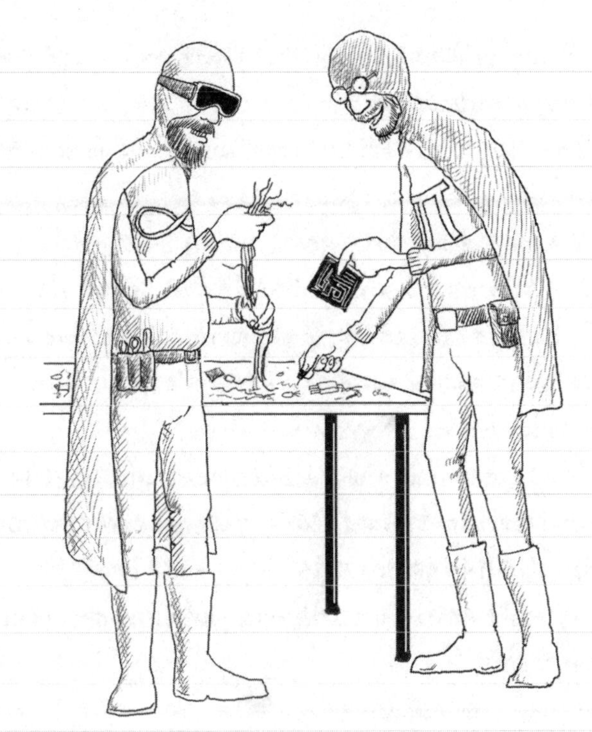

store in the Castle Leys area on Thursday. We're going to stop their little plan.'

'Yay!' I shouted. 'Justice!'

'Lame,' murmured Amazagirl.

'I'm going to lay tacks along the road leading to the store's window,' said Mrs Amazing.

'I'm going to dress up as a policeman and divert innocent motorists away from the danger,' said Mr Amazing.

'I'm going to remotely lock the doors of their van with this,' said Doctor Infinity. He picked up a black plastic square and flicked a switch on the side. 'And then I'm going to lower the windows with this.' He pressed a button on the front.

'Then I'm going to fire these at the criminals,' said Pi. He picked up a dart gun with a long barrel and slotted a syringe in the end of it. 'They contain enough ketamine to knock out a horse.'

'When the criminals have been neutralized, I'm going to tie them up and leave them for the police,' said Dan, holding up some thick ropes. 'They'll probably still get off scot-free, knowing our feeble law enforcers. But it will send a message to the guy who's really behind all this stuff. He runs all the criminal gangs in this town and he's known as Vercetti.'

I realized Dan hadn't assigned me a role, so I fumbled through my utility belt. 'I could shine my torch into the van,' I said. 'To make sure you're aiming the dart correctly.'

Pi flicked a switch on the top of the dart gun and a bright white light shone down the barrel.

'Oh,' I said. I lifted my tape measure off my utility

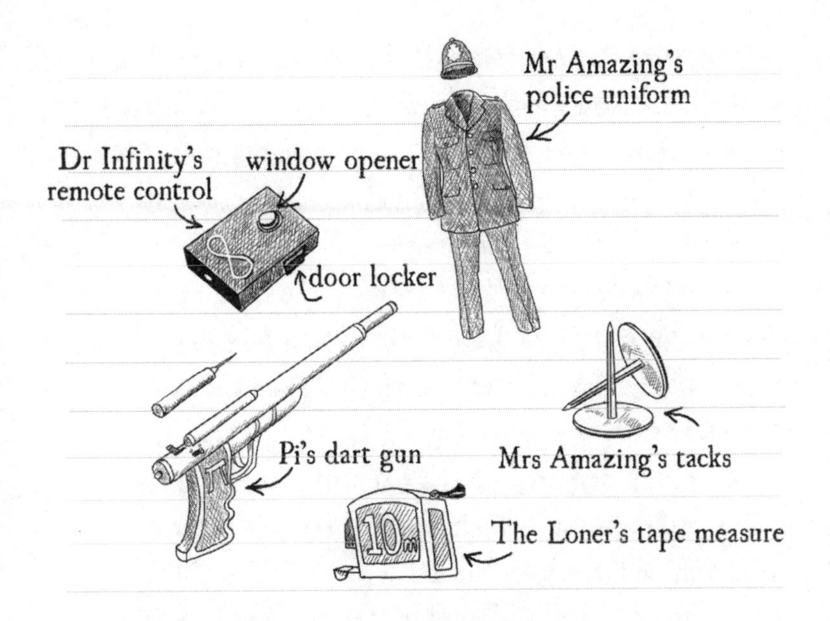

belt. 'I could measure the distance from the window to the road, to make sure you put the tacks in the right place.'

'Er ...' said Army Dan. 'Yeah, why not?'

WEDNESDAY 3RD FEBRUARY

I can't believe I'm going to fight some actual criminals tomorrow. I knew I'd make a brilliant superhero but I never dreamed I'd get so far so soon. It proves I'm made for it.

All that time I wasted in the chess club and the

role-playing games club when I should have been fighting crime. It's my destiny.

Tomorrow is going to be amazing – I can already see it.

THURSDAY 4TH FEBRUARY

I spent this evening looking through my *Ratman* comics for inspiration. I keep all my back issues in clear bags backed by cardboard, and only take them out on special occasions.

Ratman has been going since 1938. He initially battled local crime bosses using weapons of his own invention, but he soon began to fight more flamboyant baddies such as Crossword Clue and Panthergirl. A television show of the comic was made in the 1960s, but it was camp and over-the-top and proper Ratman fans like me don't regard it as canon.

Comics are as serious as Victorian novels, Shakespeare plays and classical symphonies and it makes my blood boil when people think they're just disposable trash for kids.

Mum thinks I'll eventually grow out of comics, but she's wrong. Whenever I go into a proper comic shop I see lots of middle-aged men who are just as excited about them as me. When I'm older I'm going to be just like them. Except hopefully I'll smell a bit nicer.

The seriousness of comics was shown in the 1980s when writer Thurston Baxton took over the *Ratman* title. He turned Ratman into a complex character

who spent ages on top of tall buildings pondering the nature of good and evil before beating baddies up. These comics inspired the recent *Ratman* movie series by acclaimed director Crispin Canterbury, which is so serious you can't hear what the actors are saying properly.

My evening of looking at my *Ratman* back issues has fully prepared me to get out there and battle some criminals. Now I'm just waiting for Mum and Dad's snoring to start so I can jump on the Lonerbike and race over to Dan's house.

Just heard them. Here goes!

FRIDAY 5TH FEBRUARY

I stayed off school today and pretended I had flu. I'm feeling better now, so I'm going to write down everything I can remember about the mission.

I arrived at Dan's house just as everyone was piling into the van. Mr Amazing read my name out, waited for me to say 'present' and ticked me off his list.

I squeezed onto the wooden bench running down the left side of the vehicle. Amazagirl was next to me, but she didn't look up from her phone when I tried to chat to her about how exciting it all was. Opposite us,

Doctor Infinity was fiddling with the phone jammer while Pi typed on a small laptop.

We parked a few metres down from the electronics store and I got out and performed my duty. I heroically stretched my tape measure out from the edge of the store's shop into the road. Pi had estimated it would take eighty metres for the criminals' van to come to a stop, so I extended my tape measure to its full extent eight times and marked the place with a piece of chalk every time it was fully stretched out. Finally, I traced an X on the floor and Mrs Amazing came out and scattered the tacks across the road next to it.

Mr Amazing put his police jacket on and went to divert the traffic, and Doctor Infinity and Pi snuck into an alleyway with their remote control and dart gun. Dan disappeared into the shadows on the other side of the street, while Amazagirl stayed in the van and looked at her phone. I'm not sure why she came, really. She didn't seem very eager to battle crime.

I hung around next to the van, grasping my tape measure in case anyone needed anything else measuring. As I was listening out for the van, I heard loud voices coming from the alleyway. I peered into the

darkness. Doctor Infinity and Pi were being hassled by a gang of drunk men. One of them was pulling Doctor Infinity's cape while another was trying to snatch the dart gun from Pi.

'Give me that gun,' shouted one of the drunk men. 'I want to kill a pigeon.'

I ran over and threw a Lonersnap to the ground to get their attention.

'I am The Loner and I demand you clear the area for your own safety,' I shouted.

'How come it says "The Loser" on the back of your costume?' asked one of the men.

'It was a spelling error,' I said. 'But that's not important. What's important is that you go now before things get dangerous.' I threw two more Lonersnaps to the floor to show how serious I was.

'Things are already dangerous for you losers,' said another of the men. In the gloom I spotted him punching Doctor Infinity in the stomach.

Doctor Infinity groaned and then shouted, 'Grab this, Loner.' A black box spun out of the alley towards me and I caught it with my right hand.

'Take over,' shouted Pi. The dart gun flew from the alley and I caught it with my left hand.

I tried to get over my shock at catching the objects one after another. I can't usually catch a tennis ball when I have both hands free.

I looked down at the remote control and dart gun and began to realize what was happening. The most important part of the mission had been entrusted to me. It was all up to me now.

I heard wheels screeching at the bottom of the road.

'Go!' shouted Pi. 'Quick!'

I turned to see a white van speeding towards the electronics store. There was a loud pop as the tyres hit the tacks and the vehicle skidded across the road. It listed to the side and nearly tipped over before coming to a stop.

This was it. My chance to make the mission a success. I sprinted towards the van and flicked the switch on the side of the remote. I heard a click coming from the van. Inside I saw a man wearing a mask grabbing the inside door handle. It stayed shut.

Good. I'd completed the first part of my mission. I just needed to focus and I could do the rest.

I pressed the button on the front of the remote for a second and the window slid down part way. The

masked man was screaming at me, but I paid no attention. It was time to hit the baddies with some vengeance.

I stuffed the remote control under my arm and gripped the dart gun. The masked man's arm shot out of the window and scrabbled around for the outside handle. I pulled the trigger and a dart flew out. It bounced off the lowered window and sped to the ground.

I stepped nearer to get a better shot. This time the dart deflected upward and arced to the ground behind me.

I stepped closer again. This time the dart bounced off the metal frame of the window and flew straight back at me. There was a sharp stinging in my neck and my head began to feel really heavy. I knew I was doing

something really important and needed to concentrate. But I also had a really strong feeling that going to sleep would be a good idea.

And that's all I remember.

SATURDAY 6TH FEBRUARY

I think the tranquilizer has completely worn off now but I might stay in bed anyway, just to make sure.

When I came round from the dart, it was morning and I was lying on a sofa in Dan's basement. He told me the mission had worked out fine. After I'd collapsed, he'd grabbed the gun and fired darts into the van. He'd aimed perfectly both times and knocked both the robbers out. He'd fought off the drunken men attacking Doctor Infinity and Pi while Mrs Amazing had carried me back to our van. They'd left the criminals and tipped off the police, who'd arrived soon after.

I managed to prop myself up on the sofa and Dan gave me a bottle of Coke. I was halfway through it when I realized it was half past six and I needed to get back home before Mum and Dad woke up.

I leapt onto the Lonerbike and cycled home as fast as I could, which wasn't very. I was so dazed from the

tranquilizer that I kept zigzagging from side to side. I was lucky it was still too early for many other cars or pedestrians to be about.

I got home, tied up my bike, climbed to my room and got into bed just in time to hear my parents' alarm going off.

I was tired, hot and pale. At least convincing them I had the flu wasn't a problem.

SUNDAY 7TH FEBRUARY

I felt much better this morning, so I decided to take a walk in Edgeley Park. A girl walking a golden Labrador looked over at me and said, 'Hi, Loser!'

'It's The Loner,' I said. 'Not The Loser.'

Then I realized what she'd said. My secret identity had been discovered! How had this happened? Was she working for the criminal gang? Was she about to set the dog on me? It didn't look like a very vicious dog, but that might have been part of the disguise.

'Who sent you?' I asked. 'How do you know about me?'

'It's me,' said the girl. 'Amy Gibson. My parents call me "Amazagirl", but they also think Max is

called "Amazadog", so I wouldn't take any notice of them.'

I stuck my fingers in my ears and said, 'Don't reveal your secret identity! It could compromise our missions!'

'Our missions are already compromised because they're run by a total psycho,' she said. 'My parents are way out of their depth with Dan and so are you. I used to think their historical battle recreation society was bad, but at least they only dragged me along to that in the daytime.'

I grabbed my face and remembered I wasn't wearing my mask. 'How did you even recognize me?'

'Because it's obviously you,' she said. 'Covering the top half of your face and putting on a deep voice that makes you cough isn't a great disguise, you know.'

I couldn't believe it. All Astonishingboy has to do is put on a pair of glasses to disguise himself as a mild-mannered reporter. I use a proper mask and it has no effect!

'I think we should stop this conversation,' I said. 'It could turn out to be very dangerous. Let's never speak about it again.'

'Fine,' she said. 'Whatever, Josh.'

MONDAY 8TH FEBRUARY

It turns out my secret identity isn't quite as secret as I thought. Apparently Dan checked my wallet when I was tranquilized on Thursday.

Amy says I shouldn't worry because they all know each other's identities anyway. Dan is called Dan Marshall and he used to be in the army before starting his own hydraulic equipment company. A few years ago he sold it and put his money into fighting crime.

Doctor Infinity and Pi are two mathematics postgraduates from the university called Mike and Nick. Dan pays them a small wage to develop crime-fighting equipment for him.

Amy's parents are called Malcolm and Alice Gibson and they live in one of the nice houses that back onto the park. Dan recruited them when he spotted them cleaning graffiti from an underpass with their costumes on. He used the same method of bundling them into his van and driving them back to his basement, which they thought was too dramatic.

They won't let Amy stay at home alone at night so she has to come too. She hates being a superhero

because she thinks the police are under enough pressure without meddling idiots in fancy dress, and also because her costume makes her look fat.

She should be pleased her parents have a cool hobby to bring her along to – Henry's parents used to take him line dancing.

She reckons Dan is annoyed with me for messing things up on the mission, so I'll have to make it clear to him that I intend to do much better in future.

TUESDAY 9TH FEBRUARY

Today I made a mistake that was even more painful than knocking myself out with a tranquilizer. I admitted to Henry that I'd joined the League.

He sat next to me in English and asked me over and over again why I was absent on Friday. Eventually the penny dropped and he asked if I'd tired myself out fighting crime. I told him it was really serious and I couldn't say any more, which he took as proof.

I realized I'd have to tell the truth just to shut him up. At lunchtime I took him to the far corner of the playing field and admitted I'd joined a league of costumed vigilantes. I said it was top secret and I'd be in great danger if anyone ever found out.

So how did Henry react to this serious news? By swearing on his life to never breathe a word to anyone? By tapping the side of his nose and changing the subject? No. He held his fist out and ran around shouting, 'Superhero league!' What a brilliant way to keep a secret.

When he'd finally calmed down, he asked when he could come along to a meeting. I told him that our leader had decreed no one else could ever join again.

It wasn't easy for me to tell such a blatant lie, but

at least it made him shut up. Instead of running around the school and shouting, he sat down on a bench and stared at the floor.

I felt bad, but what could I do? Bringing someone as excitable as Henry along on a crime-fighting mission would put us all in danger. The only real winners would be the criminals.

WEDNESDAY 10TH FEBRUARY

I turned up early for the League meeting to apologize to Dan for messing things up on the mission. He said it was fine, but his fists were clenched and the veins in his forehead were bulging, so I'm sure he was just trying to make me feel better.

While we waited for the others, I read the framed newspaper articles in his hallway. Some of them were about major stories:

MILLION-POUND DRUG SEIZURE IN LOCAL WAREHOUSE

STOLEN SAFETY DEPOSIT BOXES RETURNED TO BANK

OFF-LICENCE ROBBERS JAILED

Others were much less serious:

CHEESE-SHOP VANDAL GETS COMMUNITY SERVICE

DUCK RESCUED FROM FROZEN LAKE

WOMAN REUNITED WITH MISLAID HAT

'Were all these crimes foiled by the League?' I asked.

'Kind of,' said Dan. 'Some of them date to the time before the East Dudchester League of Costumed Vigilantes merged with the Central Region Masked Crime-Fighters Society. Doctor Infinity, Pi and myself were the East Dudchester League of Costumed Vigilantes. We tackled things like robberies, police corruption and gang violence. The Amazing family were the Central Region Masked Crime-Fighters Society and they focused on stuff like this.'

He tapped one of the newspaper articles, which read, 'MISSING HOOVER ATTACHMENT FOUND.'

'I don't understand,' I said. 'You three were solving really important crimes and they were doing trivial stuff. Why did you want to merge with them?'

MISSING HOOVER ATTACHMENT FOUND

'If someone has made up their mind to become a masked vigilante, I can't stop them,' said Dan. 'And it would be too dangerous to let them run around on their own. The only answer is to accept all would-be crime-fighters into the League, no matter how incompetent they are and how likely they are to mess things up on important missions.' His face had gone red and his forehead veins were bulging again.

I was about to mention that I had a friend who also wanted to be a costumed vigilante, but I'm glad I stopped myself. No doubt he'd have to accept Henry into the League too if he knew about him. I'll have to be sure never to mention him.

'I've had to put my foot down with the Amazing family a few times, though,' said Dan. 'Mr Amazing wanted his dog to join the League at one point. He tried to set it on a shoplifter, but it just ran after a squirrel.'

Dan said he had only ever rejected one costumed vigilante from the League. He was called Tyler but said his name was Flamestorm and that he could produce fire from his fingertips. Whenever they took him on missions, he'd just set fire to things with his

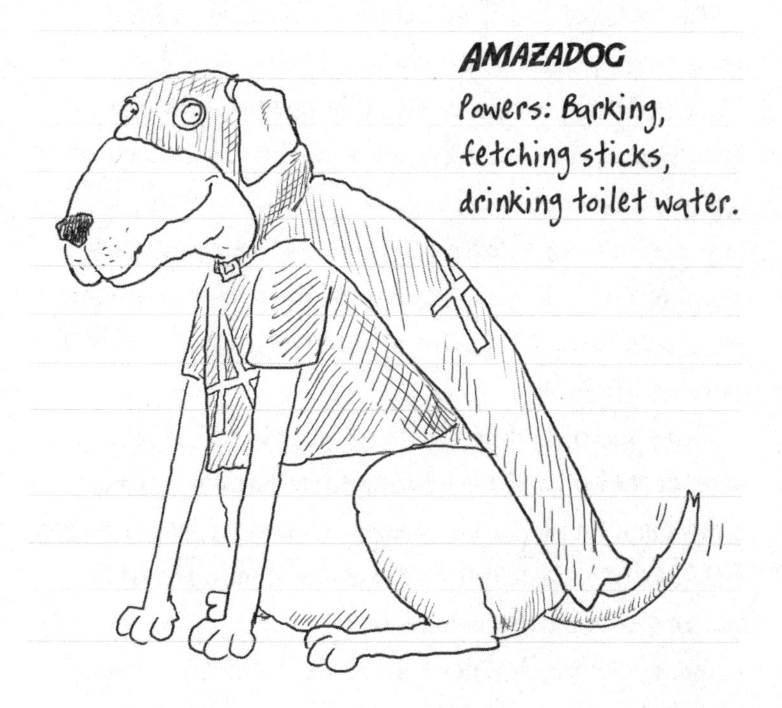

cigarette lighter. He ended up in prison for arson shortly after Dan kicked him out, so he reckons he made the right decision.

I also asked Dan about all his bottles of water. He said he never drinks tap water or even brushes his teeth with it because the government put fluoride in it to control our thoughts. He said he once drank some by mistake, and the words 'OBEY',

'CONFORM' and 'STAY ASLEEP' flashed up in his mind all night.

I'd better get Mum and Dad to buy me bottled water from now on. I definitely don't want that to happen to me.

The others arrived soon after and we went down to the basement. Dan congratulated them on the mission before revealing the good news: that there's still lots of crime to fight.

Doctor Infinity has been looking into the local crime boss Vercetti, and he's managed to hack his phone calls and record his voice for the first time. He hopes eventually to track him down so we can confront him, but in the meantime we're going to foil a robbery he's planning for Monday next week. He's getting some of his men to rob a truck delivering computers to the warehouse of a huge technology firm and we're going to stop him.

I immediately volunteered to do tons of heroic fighting to make up for my performance on Thursday. There was an awkward silence before Dan told me my duty would be to take the register.

The register? I should be taking down tough criminals, not names. Just because I tranquilized

myself last time doesn't mean I'm going to do it again.

THURSDAY 11TH FEBRUARY

Henry was waiting outside school for me this morning. He asked if I'd rethought my position on letting him join the League. I told him it wasn't up to me, but he got really angry and said he wanted to officially break up as friends.

When we first made friends at the age of seven, he made us chant, 'Make friends, make friends, never never break friends.'

You'd think he would have grown out of that sort of thing, but today he made us chant again and say, 'Break friends, break friends, never never make friends.'

He then wandered into school, presumably to find a new gang. I'm sure he'll be back when he finds out the boys from the football team don't own any back issues of *Steel Guy* and the cool gang don't care who'd win in a fight between Astonishingboy and Ratman.

FRIDAY 12TH FEBRUARY

Henry stopped me in the corridor today to tell me that he doesn't care about my crime-fighting league because he's joined a different one instead. He says they're called the Awesome Crusaders and they recruited him last night when he was running around the cinema car park with his costume on. Apparently the league contains a superhero who can pause time, another who can move objects with his mind and another who can fire lasers from his eyes.

I think our league would know if there was another in town, and I think everyone in the entire world would know if someone could really shoot lasers from their eyes or move objects with their thoughts.

But I suppose it's better to leave Henry to his little fantasies while I get on with the real business of protecting the town. It's a shame he has to make silly things up to compete with me, but at least it keeps him away from serious danger.

UPDATE

We had the school Valentine's Day post this afternoon and I didn't get a single card. Every year, we can

anonymously send cards to each other to raise money for charity. I usually get one card, but today I got nothing.

I think all the girls must sense there's something dangerous and forbidden about me now I've become a

superhero. I expect soon they'll all be swooning over pictures of The Loner and I won't be able to admit he's me.

'If only we could meet a boy as cool and handsome as The Loner,' they'll say, and I'll look on in silent frustration, putting their safety above my own happiness.

Henry got a card for the first time and I heard him boasting about it from the row behind me. He can boast all he likes. I have the satisfaction of knowing I'm a real superhero, and that's something he'll never have.

UPDATE

I've just thought of a more worrying explanation. Maybe Henry is the one who's been sending me Valentine's cards so I wouldn't get upset about not getting any. And now we've broken friends he sent one to himself instead.

SATURDAY 13TH FEBRUARY

There's a new superhero movie out today called *Steel Guy IV*. I usually go to the cinema with Henry whenever a new one opens. We go to the day's first 3D showing, sit on the front row and get a pizza afterwards to discuss where the film stands in our all-time top superhero movies. Henry always puts it at number one in his list, even if it's something awful like *Ratman Forever*, which had terrible effects, a badly designed Ratmobile and a lame romantic subplot the studio forced them to include.

I really wanted to see *Steel Guy IV*, but I couldn't ask Henry now we've officially broken friends. I was tempted to go on my own, but then I thought Henry might be there too and it would be really awkward.

Also, someone else from school might have seen me and teased me. I know that I'm meant to be The Loner

and live outside normal rules, but I'd still feel a little ashamed about going to the cinema on my own.

In the end, I gave it a miss. It would probably be really boring for me to watch a superhero movie now, anyway. It would be like Mum and Dad watching a film about people driving to the grocery store.

SUNDAY 14TH FEBRUARY

At the meeting this afternoon I told everyone about my slogan, 'You're never alone when the Loner's here' and asked them to think of their own ones.

Here's what they came up with:

Army Dan – *The war on crime will never end.*

Mr and Mrs Amazing – *Fighting crime and having an amazing time.*

Amazagirl – *Shut up, I don't have one.*

Doctor Infinity – *Justice goes on forever.*

Pi – *How I wish I could overpower Pi.*

I thought Doctor Infinity had the best one. Dan's was too negative, because we could win the war on crime one day. Mr and Mrs Amazing's slogan wasn't very memorable and I didn't understand Pi's slogan until he explained that if you count the letters in each word, it gives you the number Pi to six decimal places, 3.141592.

That sort of thing might impress his maths friends, but it will go over the heads of most criminals. If they knew about smart stuff like maths they wouldn't have turned to crime in the first place.

Even if Doctor Infinity and Pi are a bit too brainy for me to fully understand, I admire their approach to fighting crime. They use technology very creatively, taking advantage of techniques the police don't know about yet. For example, when they were tackling a spate of muggings last year, they wrote a computer program to simulate the behaviour of criminals and predicted where they'd strike next. Dan used this

knowledge to patrol crime scenes and ambush the robbers.

'We were able to fight crime using the most important element of all,' said Pi.

'What's that?' asked Doctor Infinity. 'Carbon? Hydrogen? Nitrogen? Oxygen? Phosphorus? Sulphur?'

'No,' said Pi. 'The element of surprise.'

They both chuckled.

I think Mr Amazing got jealous because he started going on about the time he rescued a piglet that had escaped from a town farm. Apparently it got all the way to a garden centre before he found it. I had to pretend to be just as impressed so he didn't feel left out.

Dan then took us through his plan for the truck heist tomorrow. Sadly, I'm still only in charge of the register. I'll just have to make sure I do a good job and get promoted next time.

Doctor Infinity played us some phone calls between Vercetti and his mob that he'd intercepted. One of the gang members had a really high voice, and the contrast with Vercetti's gravelly voice made me laugh. Dan said I had to take the mission seriously or wait upstairs, so I forced myself to stop.

After the calls had finished, Dan laid out a large plan of some crossroads and placed a toy truck on them.

'The delivery truck will approach the junction,' said Dan. He placed two toy cars on either side of the truck and pushed them towards it. 'Vercetti's men plan to intercept it at 11:30 p.m. tomorrow night.'

He pulled the cars back to their original positions and then threw a load of plastic soldier figures on the plan. 'But we're going to turn up and change that.'

I was getting quite excited by this point, so I shouted 'East Dudchester League of Costumed Vigilantes (incorporating The Central Region Masked Crime-Fighters Society) assemble!'

'Just so you know, I've been looking into this tech firm,' said Amazagirl. 'And they don't even pay all their taxes. They're worse than Vercetti's gang in their way, and I don't see the point in helping them.'

Dan's face went red and the vein in his forehead bulged again. I thought he was going to shout at Amazagirl, but he just looked down at the plan and said, 'Here's what we're going to do.'

He shoved the plastic soldiers around. 'The Loner will take the register. Mrs Amazing will wait at the end of the road, before the junction, and flash her

torch when she sees the truck approaching. Mr Amazing will step out in his police uniform and divert the truck along a parallel road, away from the criminals. Doctor Infinity will simulate the noise of an approaching truck using his laptop and some large speakers. The criminals will emerge from their vehicles and Pi and myself will neutralize them with tasers.'

Pi fetched a huge black gun from the table at the far end. He explained that it fires electrodes into the criminals, sending a current through them, which stops them being able to control their muscles.

I asked Dan if I could hold it, but he refused. I can

tell they all think I'm going to tase myself because of what happened with the tranquilizer. They need to understand that was a one-off accident that could have happened to anyone.

MONDAY 15TH FEBRUARY

I'm so stoked about catching those criminals tonight. I know I don't have a very big role to play, but it's a vital one. If I didn't take the register, we'd have no way of knowing who was present, and the whole mission would fall apart.

I've looked into what Amazagirl said and lots of people seem angry about the tech firm avoiding tax. But they're not breaking the law and the criminals are, so I'm sure we're doing the right thing. If you start thinking too hard about who the real goodies and baddies are, you'll never get anything done.

UPDATE

It's now 4 a.m. I've just returned from some really intense crime-fighting.

As soon as I heard snoring from my parents' room I jumped on the Lonercycle and rode to Dan's house. I took the register while everyone was getting in the van and I did it again when everyone was getting out to show my commitment to my responsibility.

Amazagirl didn't answer either time, and it turned out she was in a foul mood because she was missing a sleepover at her friend Bethany's house.

'I can't believe you made me come on this stupid mission,' she said as she stepped out of the van.

'We've been through this before,' said Mr Amazing. He threw his fake police uniform on the ground and stuck his hands on his hips. 'If you want to protect the innocent citizens of this town, you have to put your duties first.'

'I don't want to protect the innocent citizens of this town,' said Amazagirl. 'What's the point of paying taxes to fund the police if you're just going to do their job yourself? You might as well pave roads or fix streetlights.'

'The police are too scared to do anything,' said Dan. 'And don't get me started on the criminal justice system. All these bleeding hearts banging on about the rights of criminals. What about the rights of victims?'

I felt things were getting heated so I tried taking

the register again. It didn't work. Dan kept ranting about the police, Amazagirl went on and on about how fighting crime outside the law was stupid and her parents shouted at her for being ungrateful.

I saw a couple of bright lights at the end of the road. A large truck was approaching.

'They're here!' I shouted, but the others were too wrapped up in their argument to listen. They were all standing at the side of the van, yelling into each other's faces.

'Don't you want to stop crime?' Dan asked.

'Of course,' said Amazagirl. 'But you need to address the underlying causes if you really want to tackle it.'

I knew it was down to me to save the day – Mr Amazing wasn't going to divert the truck. I'd have to do it.

I grabbed the police uniform and pulled it on. The coat was really baggy and the pants were so long I had to hitch them up at the knees.

I ran towards the truck, stopped in the middle of the road and waved my arms around. The truck pulled up in front of me and the driver

wound his window down. I walked round to his side, trying to look as authoritative as possible. Unfortunately, I tripped and fell to the floor.

I got up and wiped the gravel from my hands.

'There's been an accident,' I said. 'You'll have to turn round and find another route.'

The driver stuck his head out of the window. 'I can't see any accidents,' he said. 'Except for you falling over just then.' He peered at me. 'And aren't you a bit young to be a police officer?'

A burly man with a shaved head leaned over from the passenger seat. 'It's just a kid messing around. Let's go.'

The man's voice was very high and squeaky and didn't seem to fit his body. There was something else weird about it that I couldn't place. Then it came to me. This was the same voice we'd heard talking to Vercetti on the phone.

I needed time to process this, but I didn't have any. Why would this man have been talking to the very person who was trying to steal from him?

Of course! It was an inside job! These men knew their truck would be robbed! They must have been working with Vercetti's gang in exchange for a share of the profits. I had to act fast before they drove to the crossroads and the rest of the League risked their lives trying to help them.

'I've been sent by Vercetti,' I said. 'The police are onto us. He's called the job off.'

The driver and the man with the high voice exchanged nervous glances.

'I don't know what you're talking about,' said the driver.

'Never heard of him,' said the man with the high voice.

Nonetheless, they reversed about a hundred metres and drove away. A few minutes later, Dan's van pulled up next to me and I jumped in.

TUESDAY 16TH FEBRUARY

I'm back from school now and I want to sleep for a million years. Today passed in a haze of exhaustion and I'm just glad I didn't fall asleep on a Bunsen burner or something.

We had a very awkward journey back last night. Everyone was still in a bad mood after the argument. Dan was gripping his taser gun really tightly and I was worried he was going to fire it at the Amazing family.

They all cheered up when I told them what had happened, partly because they were pleased with my quick thinking and partly because I'd discovered it was an inside job, so it didn't matter that they'd messed up.

'We could have risked our lives to protect those drivers,' said Dan. He was clutching the taser so tightly his knuckles were white. 'It turns out they were just criminal scum like all the others.'

It felt great to be the best hero in the league for once, and trudging through today as a sleep-deprived zombie was a small price to pay.

UPDATE

We had another meeting of the League tonight, even though we were all tired, and everyone thanked me again. Dan, Mr Amazing and Mrs Amazing all apologized for letting their argument distract them.

As a result of the row, Dan has agreed that the League will try and fight the underlying causes of crime as well as criminals themselves. We're going on a special mission to combat them tomorrow night.

In the meantime, Doctor Infinity has been intercepting more of Vercetti's calls. Apparently, he's really angry with the truck drivers for backing out of the plan and he's sent his henchmen after them.

They'll probably do something horrible like set their feet in concrete and throw them in a river, but I have no sympathy. They shouldn't have got involved with crime in the first place.

At the end of the meeting, Dan announced some great news. As punishment for neglecting his duty during the mission, he's demoting Mr Amazing from deputy leader, and giving me the role instead!

I can't believe I've been made deputy leader of the The East Dudchester League of Costumed Vigilantes (incorporating The Central Region Masked Crime-Fighters Society). That would look great on my future college applications if it weren't top secret.

WEDNESDAY 17TH FEBRUARY

At lunchtime I sat alone on the bench at the edge of the playing field and brooded over my new responsibilities. But I was too excited about them to do any proper brooding.

Deputy leader! That's amazing for someone my age!

Henry sat next to me and nibbled his sandwiches. I

knew he'd come running back when he failed to make any new friends.

I was trying really hard not to tell him anything about the League, but I was so excited I couldn't keep quiet. I told him all about the truck heist and my promotion to deputy leader.

This must have made him jealous because he went off on a bizarre flight of fancy about his own imaginary league. He said they were going to fake an alien invasion of Earth to unite all the governments of the world, which is an idea he stole from *Astonishingboy* issues 736–740. If he's going to tell

ridiculous lies, he should at least avoid taking them from comics he knows I've read.

UPDATE

After school I met up with the rest of the League for our first mission to tackle the underlying causes of crime. We went for a coffee and managed to get the sofas at the back, which was quite a result. Dan didn't turn up, which was very disappointing.

Amazagirl showed us a study she'd printed from the internet that said the underlying causes of crime are poverty, poor education and bad anger management. Then we went out into the streets where people suffering from these things were most likely to be.

We found a group of young children kicking a ball around who looked as though they might be poor. Mr Amazing gave them a moving speech about how crime doesn't pay. Unfortunately, rather than listening to him, they challenged each other to hit him in the face with their ball.

Mr Amazing's lecture might not have seemed like a huge success, but maybe one day one of those children will be on the verge of committing a crime and they'll

remember the wise things he said as they aimed the ball at his head.

THURSDAY 18TH FEBRUARY

I totally forgot we had my parent–teacher interviews tonight. They were much worse than usual, and Mum and Dad seemed concerned as we drove home. I told them I was just going through a rebellious teenage phase and to prove it I undid my seat belt. Dad pulled up at the side of the road and refused to go any farther until I put it back on.

I wish I could tell them what I've really been up to. They'd be really proud to find out that not only have

I joined a costumed vigilante gang, but I've been made deputy leader.

That's much more impressive than getting a good school report. But it would worry them too much. If they won't let me ride without a seat belt, I doubt they'd be pleased to hear I'm sneaking out at night to battle criminal gangs.

FRIDAY 19TH FEBRUARY

We went back out to tackle the underlying causes of crime tonight and once again, Dan didn't show up.

This time we patrolled the bars in the town centre, looking for poorly educated people so we could persuade them not to commit crimes.

We spotted a group of men outside a bar who looked like they might fit the bill, and Pi confirmed this by asking them some basic trigonometry questions. None of them had any idea what he was going on about.

Mr Amazing began his lecture, but the men got the wrong end of the stick and thought he was accusing them of having already committed some crime. When he explained he was talking to them because they looked like they might become

criminals, they got up from their table and started pushing him.

I tried to create a distraction by throwing Lonersnaps, but this only angered the men further.

When they threatened to punch us, we took a group decision to run away and hide behind a wall. Mr Amazing announced that as well as being poorly educated, the men also had anger management issues, which meant we'd now tackled all three underlying causes of crime and could go home.

SATURDAY 20TH FEBRUARY

Massive crime alert! Doctor Infinity and Pi have intercepted more of Vercetti's calls and found his men are going to rob the bank at the top of the high street on Wednesday afternoon.

It's a huge job and Vercetti's even had to hire a technical advisor of his own. Doctor Infinity hacked a call where he was telling a man to design a machine that can change traffic lights.

Vercetti wants to trap all the other vehicles on side streets so his gang can make a clear getaway down the high street. This has made Pi really competitive and he's been working on a light-changing machine of his own. He wants to reverse the plan and block the street with traffic so the criminals can't get away. Doctor Infinity will then use his remote control to lock the doors of the truck and trap the criminals inside until the police get through.

I can't believe Vercetti has a technical advisor too. Any scientist working for the enemy must be an evil one, and if comics have taught me anything, it's that you can't trust evil scientists. One minute they'll be designing a traffic light machine, the next they'll be developing a formula to make extra limbs sprout from their body.

I've been given the responsibility of helping Dan

clear innocent pedestrians out the way, and the Amazing family have been given nothing to do but take the register and stay as far back as possible. These roles fairly reflect my promotion and Mr Amazing's demotion, but he got offended and demanded more responsibility. Dan said he could look out for escaped farm animals, which only made him more annoyed.

Amazagirl went off on another one of her rants, probably because she was jealous too.

'I've got a better idea,' she said. 'Why don't we just stay away and let the criminals rob the bank? Even if they succeed, insurance companies will cover it. No individuals will lose any money.'

'This is about doing what's right and protecting the innocent,' said Dan. He pressed his hands to his temples. 'That's what we vowed to do when we started this league.'

'If we want to protect the innocent, it would be better to stay away,' said Amazagirl. 'They're much more likely to get hurt if a bunch of vigilantes show up. The worst that will happen if we let the robbery go ahead is the bank might have to pay slightly more insurance in the future, and why would that matter? Everyone hates banks these days.'

'It's about justice!' shouted Dan. His face was pretty much purple now.

Dan was so angry we all had to leave while he used his gym, and I gave Amazagirl a stern glare on the way out. We'd been having a very enjoyable meeting about an important mission, and she'd ruined it for everyone again.

SUNDAY 21ST FEBRUARY

Amazagirl's rant has been on my mind today. I know she only said it to annoy Dan, but it did sort of make sense. I looked online and it turns out she was telling the truth about the insurance companies paying out when banks are robbed.

It certainly puts my old *Astonishingboy* comics in a different light. In issue 871, he destroys an entire neighbourhood just to foil a bank robbery. He hurls cars and trucks at Vex Valour's henchmen, smashing up countless office blocks and shopping malls.

In other words, he causes millions of dollars of damage to innocent people's property just to save the bank a few thousand dollars. Maybe it would have been better if he hadn't bothered at all.

But if we let one criminal gang get away with robbing a bank, everyone would do it and then where would we be?

Hang on a minute, I think I'm having a moral dilemma, like in Thurston Baxton's controversial run on the *Ratman* comic. I need to stand on top of a tall building and do some brooding.

UPDATE

The nearest tall buildings I could find were the high-rise blocks on the edge of Raven's Green. I climbed up the stairs of one and was about to open the door to the roof when I noticed it was alarmed. I tried brooding in the stairwell instead, but the smell of urine put me off.

I didn't really need to brood anyway, because I'd already made my mind up not to worry.

I remembered *Ratman* issue 764. It starts with him as a young superhero rescuing a child from an apartment block fire. At the end we find out that the child he rescued grew up to become his nemesis the Electric Eel.

At first he wonders if he really should have left the child to burn. But after a spot of rooftop brooding he decides it was the right thing to do, even if it had bad consequences. Superheroes must always do what's right and avoid worrying about what will come.

Stealing is wrong, and we must prevent it because we're on the side of right. If we brood too much over complicated things, it will distract us from our duty.

That's enough brooding. It's time to dish out some justice.

MONDAY 22ND FEBRUARY

Henry sat next to me in physics this morning and asked me for the latest news about the League. I wish I'd never told him anything now. I only blabbed about it because I was excited about becoming deputy leader. I told him I could never speak of it again.

I distracted him by asking him about his imaginary league. He spouted some rubbish about how they were going to save the world from nuclear attack by hurling a stray missile into a wormhole. He stole that idea from *Steel Man* issue 374, by the way.

TUESDAY 23RD FEBRUARY

This is all getting really serious. I'm going to be on the scene of an actual bank robbery tomorrow. The closest I've come to witnessing such a serious crime before was when I saw *Steel Guy II* in IMAX 3D.

This will be the first League mission during school hours, so I'm going to have to fake a sick note. That feels quite wrong, even though I'm doing it for the greater good.

The criminals are going to rob the bank shortly after it opens at 9.30 a.m. I'm glad, because this means all the crime-fighting will be over by the time Mum and Dad return from work at half five. The last thing I want is to let the criminals escape because it's my turn to set the table for dinner.

I'm going to have to put my costume on in Dan's bathroom, which will be inconvenient. I'd feel much better if I could turn up to his house as The Loner, but I can't think of anywhere to get changed along the way.

Astonishingboy changes in public callboxes and the revolving doors of office blocks, but neither would be good for me. There aren't any callboxes left in our town, and I really can't see the whole revolving door thing working.

WEDNESDAY 24TH FEBRUARY

Dan looked annoyed when I arrived at his door without my costume this morning, and pushed me into the bathroom to change.

Mrs Amazing said Amazagirl wasn't coming because it was a school day, which enraged Dan further. I was glad she wasn't there, though. You need to think positively when you're battling crime, and that's hard if you're surrounded by moaners.

We climbed into the van and Pi switched on his traffic light changing device. 'Let's get out there and Tungsten, Holmium, Oxygen, Phosphorus, Arsenic, Sulphur!'

Doctor Infinity snorted out a laugh and I tried to join in, but I must have looked confused.

'Pi just spelt out the words "Whoop Ass" in chemical symbols,' said Doctor Infinity. 'He likes to tell chemistry jokes periodically.'

'And they usually get no reaction,' said Pi.

They both started laughing again. I felt slightly better about doing badly on my test the other week, because I was clearly learning some science stuff now.

We arrived outside the bank at twenty past nine and took our positions. Dan and Doctor Infinity lurked

on either side of the building, while I waited across the street and Pi went off to change the traffic lights. Meanwhile, Mr and Mrs Amazing took the register and stood really far back from the bank, folding their arms and scowling.

The doors of the bank opened and a few people wandered in. I hoped these innocent, unsuspecting members of the public wouldn't get caught up in the deadly events to follow. Or that they would, but I'd rescue them in a really heroic way.

A white truck sped down the road and slammed to a halt outside the bank, in a restricted parking zone. The criminals had already broken parking laws. They clearly meant business.

A side door flew open and two men with stockings over their heads leapt out and ran into the bank. They were carrying what looked like shotguns, but I tried not to think about them. I was pretty sure Henry's mum hadn't used shotgun-proof Lycra for my costume. Anyway, I wasn't here to worry about my own safety. I was here to protect the public.

The only member of the public on my side of the street was an old lady carrying a few heavy shopping bags. I told her to evacuate the area, but she

started hitting me with her bags, so I got out her way. She didn't look like she needed much protection anyway.

I heard shouting from further down the street. I turned round and saw Pi yelling at a man with glasses and long hair who was standing next to a set of traffic lights and clutching a small plastic box.

This must have been Vercetti's technical advisor. He didn't look much like a mad scientist. Instead of

wearing a white coat and laughing at some bubbling liquid, he had long puny arms sticking out of his black t-shirt and was hunched over his remote control device.

He shoved Pi and Pi pulled his hair in retaliation. He yanked Pi's cape, almost dragging him over. Pi swiped the man's glasses off and threw them to the ground. One of the lenses popped out and rolled into the gutter.

This was turning into a full-on nerd fight, like the one Henry had with a boy called Alan at the role-playing games club. We managed to settle that one with a twenty-sided dice, but this wasn't going to be over anytime soon.

This was partly because they'd both worked themselves into a rage and partly because they kept missing each other when they tried to strike. I doubted the technical advisor could have done much damage to Pi even if he had sprouted extra limbs.

I ran over to the brawling dweebs and scooped Pi's remote control from the ground. I examined the black box as I rushed over to the first set of traffic lights. It seemed simple enough. There was a red

MISS!
FAIL!

button and a green button. I just needed to turn all the lights green and gridlock the road with traffic, so the criminals couldn't escape.

I pointed the box at the lights and pressed the green button. They turned green right away. I repeated this with the lights on the other side of the street.

I sprinted down the street, switching all the lights to green. I forced myself to go as fast as I could, knowing that I needed to get through them all before the criminals were out. I had to jam the road completely to foil their getaway.

I was almost at the end of the street when I heard the first smash. A red sports car had crashed into the side of a truck and I could hear blaring horns. The drivers got out and yelled in each other's faces.

There was a screech of brakes and I turned to see a green car crunch into a delivery van. On the crossing opposite, a motorbike slammed into the side of a taxi. The biker slid across the floor, got up and pounded the driver's window.

That's when I realized why Pi had included the red button on his remote. Every time I switched a set of

lights to green, I should have turned the ones next to them red. By letting drivers from all directions speed across the junctions, I'd done more than gridlock the street; I'd turned it into a scene of car crash carnage. Whoops.

At the top of the street, the robbers rushed out of the bank, bundled into their vehicle and drove forward. They got just a few metres before getting trapped behind a bus and a flatbed truck that had slammed into each other.

I saw Doctor Infinity circling the criminals' truck with his remote control.

So our plan was pretty much working. Give or take the odd car crash and nerd fight, the mission was going fine.

THURSDAY 25TH FEBRUARY

My parents kept the news on while we were eating last night, which is rare for them. They have a weird thing about us sitting around the table and eating with no television or phones. But last night they were too hooked on the news to turn it off.

Watching coverage of the robbery made me really nervous, and it was even more of a struggle than usual to force down Dad's tuna pasta bake.

I kept expecting them to announce that someone had been killed in one of the crashes and I'd be driven mad with guilt, like in *Ratman* issue 616 where he fails to save the burning hospital so he can capture Crossword Clue.

But the only civilian injury they reported was a motorcyclist who broke his wrist. I think I'll be able to cope with the guilt about that. One of them nearly went over my foot with his front wheel once, so if anything it counts as vengeance.

I think I got away with my little traffic mistake,

as none of the reports mentioned mysterious masked figures messing with the lights. Everyone seems to believe the car crashes happened because of the robbery and I'm happy to let them think it.

The mission was a big success overall. The robbers were caught and the money was returned. The technical advisor fled the scene as soon as things went wrong for the criminals, which means Pi won his first ever fight.

As for the collateral damage, it was nothing compared to the destruction unleashed on New York when Astonisingboy fought the Typhoon, or the damage inflicted on downtown LA when Steel Guy fought fifty clones of himself. So by superhero standards we did pretty well.

FRIDAY 26TH FEBRUARY

Henry saw the robbery on the news and he suspects the League were involved. He sat next to me in English and kept asking me why I was off school on Wednesday. For someone who can't open a mayonnaise sachet without spurting it into his eyes and having to go to the school nurse, he can be quite clever sometimes.

To distract him from his suspicions, I reignited our

old dispute about who would win in a fight between Ratman and Astonishingboy. We argued about this for over three hours on the way back from the science museum last year.

The answer is Astonishingboy, obviously. He can fly, he can spit out deadly fire or ice, he can read minds, he can duplicate himself and he can throw his logo at enemies and trap them inside it. He's basically an alien who landed on our planet and stuck around to protect us.

Ratman, on the other hand, is a rich guy with lots of expensive stuff. There's nothing supernatural in his universe if you believe an umbrella can be modified into a working helicopter, which I do.

Every time I explain one of Astonishingboy's powers to Henry, he comes up with a gadget to beat it. There's never any scientific basis for these inventions; he just makes up something stupid like the fire-guarder, the ice-melter or the mind-protector and thinks he's won the argument.

I even brought in my rare copy of *Astonishingboy* issue 273 once, which proves he can explode objects by staring at them. That should have killed the argument for good, because he could instantly blow up any device Ratman built. But Henry spent all afternoon designing a force field that would cancel it out.

I realized he was incapable of having a serious conversation on the subject and had vowed never to discuss it with him again. But I broke my vow today and forced myself to listen to his ridiculous opinions. It was a small price to pay to draw his attention away from the League.

SATURDAY 27TH FEBRUARY

Amazagirl turned up to our League meeting today, unfortunately. She stays away when there's actual danger, then comes along to criticize us in the safety of Dan's house.

She went on and on about how we'd messed up the mission and caused lots of damage. She called my little mishap with the traffic lights idiotic, which was harsh. I'd had to think on my feet because Pi got sidetracked by his nerd fight. I think I did pretty well in the circumstances.

She told Dan we should stop going on such dangerous missions, but he said that would send out the wrong message to criminals. Instead of keeping us away from danger, he's going to give us technology training so we're all better equipped to cope with mishaps on future missions.

Amazagirl wasn't happy, but I'm really looking forward to it. If I add technological expertise to my natural abilities, I'm bound to become one of the greatest superheroes in the world. Plus, knowing about technology is a useful skill in the modern workplace, so it will give me something to fall back on if we eradicate crime and I have to change career.

SUNDAY 28TH FEBRUARY

We were let into Doctor Infinity and Pi's secret workshop this afternoon for our technology training. I expected it to be a gleaming laboratory with chrome surfaces and bright lighting, but it was a windowless shed under Dan's garden that smelled of stale food.

He built it a few years ago when he became convinced North Korea were about to drop a nuclear bomb on our town. He locked himself in and survived on baked beans for four weeks before emerging to find that not only was the town safe, but his neighbour was blocking the driveway with his campervan. It was one of the most disappointing days of his life.

Dan didn't join us for the technology training, because he knows it all already, but the Amazing family all came. Amazagirl sulked as if she were on a school trip to the ironing museum. That proves she's moody all the time, because there was some really great stuff in there.

There was a large beige machine at the back of the room and I asked Pi about it.

'It's an X-ray machine we got from a hospital,' he said. 'Dan wanted us to build a gadget that could give him X-ray vision, but it turned out X-ray vision isn't very useful for catching criminals. Unless they're small, made of metal and have been accidentally swallowed.'

There was a brilliant thing that looked like a red suit of armour and I asked about that.

'It was meant to protect Dan against enemy attacks,' said Doctor Infinity. 'We were supposed to transmit instructions into the headset while he was battling villains. But the suit was too heavy and the signal kept

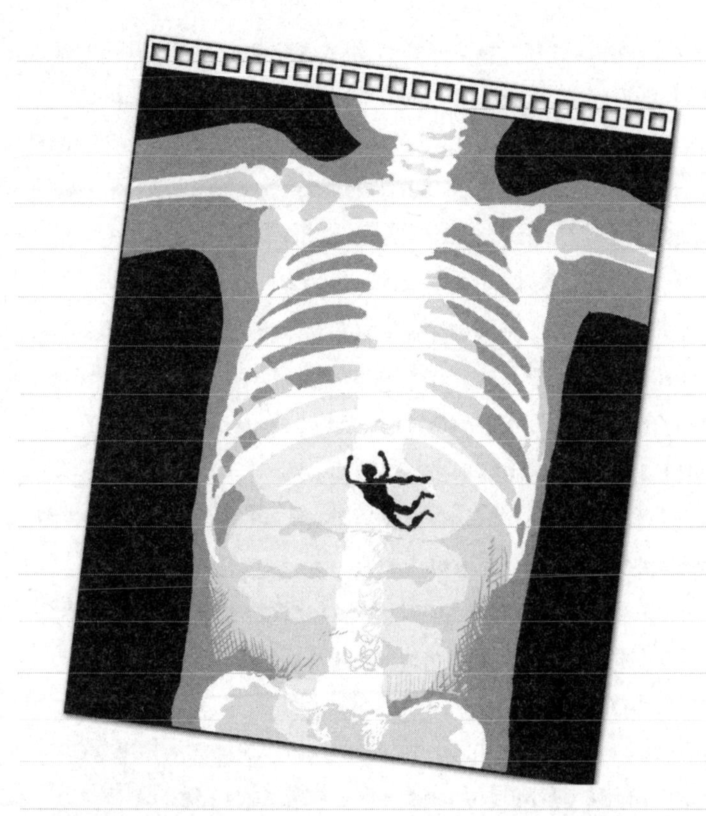

cutting out. He had to keep climbing trees to get reception and it made him too tired to fight crime.'

Best of all was a metal backpack with two large rockets attached. 'That's a jetpack we developed to make Dan fly, but it was too powerful. He only tried it a few times and he ripped down so many overhead power cables that it led to a blackout across town.

Plus it caused a lot of serious fires, and there isn't much airborne crime around here anyway.'

Pi then took us through some of their more successful inventions. He showed us the remote control for locking car doors and windows, the one for controlling traffic lights, and one that could freeze elevators between floors.

After introducing each similar black plastic device, he passed them round for us to examine.

I kept looking over at the jetpack and wondering if they'd let me incorporate it into my costume. Even if I took down a few power lines and caused the odd fire it would be worth it to become an actual flying hero like Astonishingboy. I'd definitely swoop past Henry's bedroom window just to see the look on his face.

Doctor Infinity handed me another black plastic device and I prodded a large red button on the front of it. I heard a scream next to me and saw Amazagirl collapse to the floor with a tranquilizer dart in her neck.

It turned out Pi had been explaining that this was a compact dart gun and we shouldn't press any of the buttons on it. Whoops.

We had to abandon the rest of the technology training while Mr and Mrs Amazing took Amazagirl home to sleep it off.

I thought Dan would be really angry with me for failing to pay attention, but he was actually quite pleased. He said that tranquilizing Amazagirl was the most heroic thing I'd done so far.

MONDAY 29TH FEBRUARY

This morning I handed over my fake note for missing school on Wednesday and Mr Singh didn't question it. I didn't even feel nervous handing it over, which shows how far I've come. Last year I'd never have been able to give him a forged note without blurting out a confession and begging for forgiveness.

It's just as well I didn't base my superhero identity around good attendance, because I'm sure I'll have to miss many more days as my battle against crime goes on.

I really hope a massive crime doesn't happen in the school grounds, because I'll have to run away and change into my Loner costume to combat it. Everyone will think I've fled the scene in fright, when really

I'll be protecting them. It's a classic superhero problem.

UPDATE

Crime alert! Dan has found out that Vercetti's men are going to blow up the ATM outside the cinema on Friday. They're going to use a suitcase bomb to blow the front off the machine so they can grab all the money inside.

We held an emergency brainstorming session tonight to decide how we were going to thwart this fiendish

crime. Amazagirl's idea was for me to jump on top of the suitcase and sacrifice myself by taking the force of the explosion.

This was rejected, I'm pleased to report.

Dan's idea was to pour gasoline into the cash point so the bomb triggers a massive fire, leaving no money for the criminals to steal. Amazagirl pointed out that it would be less damaging just to let the thieves take the cash. She always has to spoil the fun.

Pi came up with the plan we went for. He's going to invent a device that will deactivate the suitcase bomb. It will use a 'brute-force' attack, which means it will run through all the possible passcodes until it hits the right one.

As soon as the criminals plonk their bomb in front of the ATM, we're going to grab it and render it harmless with Pi's machine. All he has to do is make sure his device is fast enough to run through all the possible combinations before the bomb goes off.

It all sounds pretty safe. I think.

Amazagirl refused to go, which was no surprise. But Mr and Mrs Amazing tried to wriggle out of it too. They said there wasn't any clear role for them in the

mission, which doesn't usually stop them tagging along and sharing in our glory. I think they're just scared because they'll be in a van with a bomb that might go off.

Dan threatened to banish them from the League if they didn't come, and I think that's only fair. You can't choose your battles against crime. You either hate it or you love it.

Mr and Mrs Amazing are just going to have to accept that being a costumed vigilante involves bigger risks than rescuing startled piglets.

TUESDAY 1ST MARCH

Okay, I'll admit it. I'm a little worried about the bomb too.

There have been a few small problems with my superhero adventures so far: I've tranquilized myself, I've tranquilized Amazagirl and a motorcyclist has broken his wrist. But that's pretty much it.

If this mission goes wrong, my head will end up in a different county from my feet and they'll have to identify me from the dental records. I trust Dan to make the right decision and I trust Pi to build a good

machine, but I also wish we'd agreed on a less risky plan. Like running away and hiding.

WEDNESDAY 2ND MARCH

I turned up early for the meeting at Dan's house today and found him sewing a layer of tinfoil into the lining of his balaclava. He said the government tries to control your mind with secret messages and the only way to shield yourself is to cover your head with tinfoil.

He offered to sew some into my mask, but I declined. I know tinfoil is good for protecting

sandwiches, but I'm pretty sure it can't be used to protect thoughts.

At any rate, Dan should be worried about deadly bomb fragments entering his head rather than government messages. Sometimes I worry about the sort of leader I'm entrusting my life to on these missions.

When everyone had arrived we went into the weapons lab to see Pi's bomb-deactivating machine in action.

Doctor Infinity rigged up a fake suitcase bomb and Pi held a small black plastic device over it. The timer on the suitcase bomb counted down from ten and green lights on Pi's device flickered as it ran through all the possible codes.

The timer of the fake bomb reached zero and the word 'BANG' flashed up on the display.

'It was working fine before,' muttered Pi. He smacked the side of the device.

Doctor Infinity set the timer for thirty seconds and they tried again. This time the machine's lights cut out halfway through.

'That'll be the batteries,' said Pi. 'I've been using it quite a lot today.'

He unscrewed a hatch on the back and replaced four

batteries. It wasn't comforting to know that they'd stand between us and death on Friday.

Next, Doctor Infinity set the timer for five minutes and Pi held his machine over it. The countdown had gone all the way down to twenty-seven seconds when it stopped and the word 'CANCELLED' flashed on the screen.

Dan started a round of applause, but my hands were trembling too much to join in.

I feel better now, though. As long as the criminals set the timer on their bomb to more than a couple of minutes and the batteries hold out on our machine, we're unlikely to be killed.

THURSDAY 3RD MARCH

I don't want to go tomorrow. I hate explosions. I once fell off my bike because I heard a car backfire. I'm not even that confident around party poppers. I'll tell Dan I have a cold and need to stay at home in case I set the bomb off by sneezing.

No. He'll know I'm lying. Or worse, he'll think the government has turned me against him and make me wrap myself in foil.

I'm just going to have to force myself to go. I

didn't get into crime-fighting for mild peril. I could eat one of the out-of-date chicken legs in the fridge if I wanted that. I got into it to risk my life for a better world.

On the positive side, knowing I might die very soon made me much braver than usual in PE today. They always put me in goal because I'm not very good at kicking the ball or running or not tripping over my legs. I usually cover my face with my hands when the ball comes near, but today I launched myself at it every time and saved tons of goals. My team still lost, but for once it wasn't my fault.

Henry raced up to me as I was walking home and started spouting nonsense about his league's plan to save Earth from an asteroid by breaking it up with a laser beam, an idea he stole from *Steel Guy* issue 236.

It's funny how he's always talking about upcoming missions and never ones he's actually done. You'd think at least one of these Earth-saving escapades would be worth reporting back on.

Henry kept questioning me about what my league was up to, but again I gave nothing away. I'll just leave

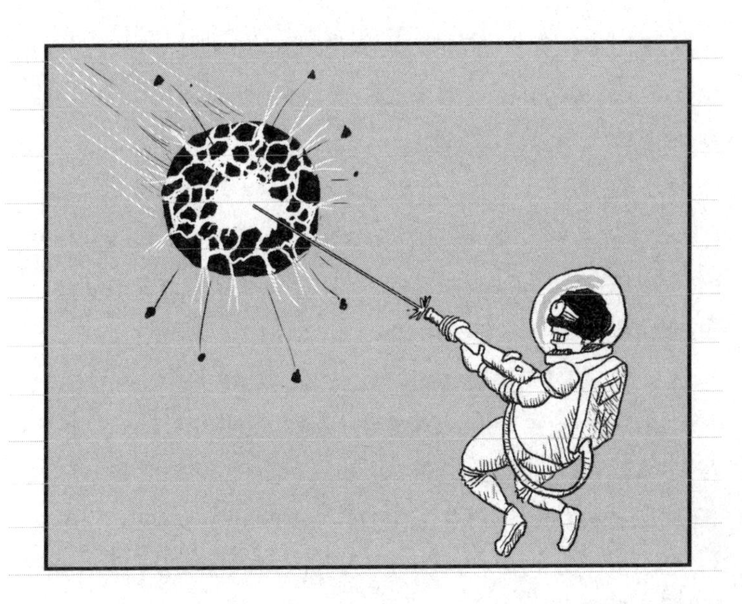

him to his harmless little fantasy world while I stick to my real and dangerous one.

FRIDAY 4TH MARCH

When we got to Dan's house he announced that Pi had made bomb-deactivating devices for all of us. So if one failed to work, there would be another five on hand.

This made me feel a little better, but as soon as he handed mine over it fell apart and the batteries sprang out onto the floor.

'You'll have to share with Mr Amazing,' said Pi, who was still screwing the back on his own device. 'I don't have time to fix it now.'

The mood was very grim as we drove to the cinema car park. I was given the task of taking the register, which was more than Mr and Mrs Amazing, who were given nothing at all to do.

Not that they complained. They were both sitting on the left-hand bench, squashing up against the side of the van with their bomb-deactivating devices held up for protection. I didn't think either were about to volunteer to take over Dan's role of grabbing the bomb and bringing it in.

Doctor Infinity parked us in front of the main entrance, while Dan talked us through the plan. For most of us, it was pretty much to stare at the bomb and hope it wouldn't go off.

The criminals sped into the car park just after midnight and pulled up outside the ATM. A bald man rushed out and placed a suitcase on the keypad of the machine. He fled back into the van and it drove to the far side of the car park.

'Let's go!' shouted Pi. 'Unlike the number on Doctor Infinity's chest, this just got real.'

Doctor Infinity drove us up to the ATM. Dan leapt out, grabbed the suitcase and brought it in. I could feel my heart hammering as he placed it on the bench next to the door and flipped it open.

Inside there was a tangle of wires, canisters and circuit boards around a counter ticking down from 2 minutes and 23 seconds.

'We can do this!' shouted Dan. That was nice to hear.

Doctor Infinity drove us out of the car park, while Pi held his device over the open case. Its green lights blinked on and off, which at least meant the batteries were working.

Dan pointed at Mr and Mrs Amazing, who were pressing themselves against the side of the van.

'You two,' he shouted. 'Get over here and be ready to use your deactivators if this one fails.' They stayed exactly where they were.

The van slowed down.

'What are you doing?' yelled Dan.

'Red light,' said Doctor Infinity. 'I can't just jump it.'

'Keep driving!' shouted Dan. 'Get us away from the residential areas and into the industrial estate. We need to minimize civilian casualties.'

By the time there was just one minute on the clock, we were at the big crossroads. By the time there were thirty seconds left, we were driving past empty office blocks.

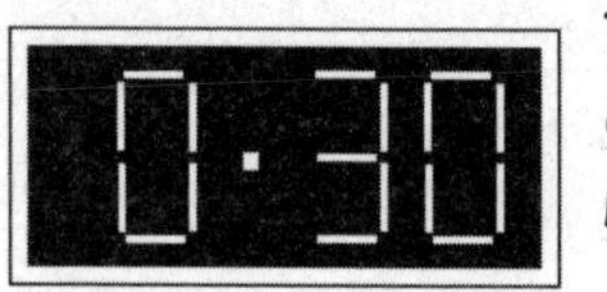

'Come on!' shouted Pi, hitting the side of his device. 'You must have found the passcode by now.'

Twenty seconds to go.

'Stop the van!' shouted Dan. 'I'll take the bomb and run away from the vehicle. You lot try and shield yourselves from the blast.'

'No!' shouted Pi. 'It's working. Leave it.'

Mr and Mrs Amazing cowered behind their devices. I didn't flinch at all, which was quite surprising. Usually an especially loud dog bark is enough to set me off. But this was so frightening it didn't feel like it was really happening.

Ten seconds to go.

'Almost there!' shouted Pi.

Six seconds to go.

Mr Amazing let out a low whimper.

Five seconds to go.

A bead of sweat trickled down Dan's forehead and dripped onto the suitcase.

Four seconds to go.

The clock stopped at 3.14 seconds and the word 'CANCELLED' flashed up on the screen.

'Look at that,' said Pi. 'It's stopped on my favourite number.'

It was a strange time to make a maths joke.

SATURDAY 6TH MARCH

I didn't get back until 4a.m. this morning. Dad woke me up at twelve and accused me of being lazy. He wouldn't have said that if he knew what I'd really been up to.

He made me empty the dishwasher as punishment. Usually I try and spice it up by giving myself a time limit, but it wasn't very exciting after last night. When you've stared death in the face, even rapidly emptying the dishwasher loses its appeal.

This afternoon I tried to rekindle my sense of risk by going for a walk without an umbrella even though it was drizzling. Then I carried back lots of heavy shopping in a single bag, which could easily have broken. This evening I even took my portable hard drive out of my computer without ejecting it safely first.

But it was no use. None of it felt dangerous anymore. Now I understand why superheroes find it so hard to fit back into ordinary life after their missions.

SUNDAY 7TH MARCH

Pi has been working on the suitcase bomb to find clues that might lead us to Vercetti. He's taken apart the explosives, the detonator, the timer and the suitcase itself so far.

Dan's really pushing him to find something, as he reckons this is our best ever chance to track down the guy who's behind all the crime in this town.

Vercetti is the criminal the local police have always wanted to find, so if we can get him it will prove costumed vigilantes are better. Everything Dan has done since he sold his business has been leading up to this, except for the four weeks he spent in the Scottish highlands surviving on berries and trying to track down Osama bin Laden, which he now admits was a mistake.

MONDAY 7TH MARCH

Henry joined me on the benches at the edge of the sports field this lunchtime. I longed to tell him I'd seen an actual bomb. It was awful to have so much excitement in my life and not be able to talk about it.

He'd only have made up something ridiculous about how he was going to rip apart a nuclear missile with his bare hands or something, but it would have been a relief to talk to someone about what happened.

I suppose this is what I signed up to when I took on a secret double life. My reward should be the safety of the public, not the glory.

A little bit of glory would be nice, though.

I took my mind off it by reigniting our old argument about the aquatic superhero Water Guy. Henry thinks he's one of the top five superheroes ever, which is just ridiculous.

I'll be the first to admit Water Guy has some decent powers. He can breathe underwater, create giant waves and communicate telepathically with marine life. So if you're a pirate, Nazi submarine captain or arsonist who works mainly on jetties, watch out. But if you're a land-based criminal, you have

nothing to worry about because Water Guy CAN'T LEAVE THE OCEAN.

Perhaps one day sea levels will rise so much that Water Guy will be the greatest hero in the world. Until then, he doesn't even belong in the top hundred.

TUESDAY 8TH MARCH

Pi has been analysing the bomb and he reckons most of the components were smuggled in from abroad. But the battery is from this country, and he thinks it might lead us to Vercetti.

It's a large, square battery made by a company called Heavy Duty. If we can find the store that sold it to the criminals, Pi might be able to hack into their records and trace the credit card used to buy it. This might lead to a false address, but if we're lucky it could lead us straight to Vercetti's headquarters.

Which means I'm back in detective mode. I much prefer detective work to sitting in a van next to a bomb that could blow me apart.

Dan has divided a map of the town into four segments and allocated one to himself, one to me, one to Mr Amazing and one to Mrs Amazing. I've got the north-east quarter. I really hope I find the battery there and it leads us to Vercetti. That way I'll have played a big part in the capture of the most notorious crime boss this town has ever known.

Come on, north-east Dudchester! We can do this!

WEDNESDAY 9TH MARCH

I had to take the Lonerbike to school today so I could patrol the north-east quarter as soon as my lessons finished. I knew that many of the shops would close at half five and I wouldn't have long to trace the battery.

At first I tried checking every single store, but then I realized this wasn't very good detective work. I asked myself what the world's greatest detective, Ratman, would do. He'd kidnap a mobster and torture them until they revealed where Vercetti was.

That option wasn't open to me, but I used my detective skills to discount some options, such as dry cleaners, furniture stores and pharmacies.

In one of the electronics stores I checked, the security guard made me open my bag to prove I wasn't stealing anything. I couldn't believe he was letting his own petty duties hold back my serious investigations.

I hadn't found any of the batteries by the time the shops were starting to close up for the night, and I was about to give up when I spotted a small shop attached to a mechanic's. I rushed inside and saw a whole display of batteries, including the exact ones I was looking for.

A man in a greasy overall stepped out and glared at me. I pointed to a set of plastic hubcaps and asked how much they were, even though the price was clearly marked.

He stared at me until I left, so he must have suspected me of shoplifting too. I think if I was a teenage petty criminal, I'd want to steal something more exciting than antifreeze.

THURSDAY 10TH MARCH

Mrs Amazing and Dan both found places selling the batteries too. One was a large hardware store and the other was a retail store on the edge of town. Mr Amazing obviously felt left out, because he started boasting about the time he rescued a hat from a tree. Which isn't exactly up there with helping to capture Vercetti.

Pi is going to follow all three leads. I know it shouldn't matter, but I really hope the criminals bought the battery from my store, because that would make me the best detective.

FRIDAY 11TH MARCH

Dan reckons he's traced Vercetti through my shop! Strike up another victory for the Loner!

Pi generated a list of addresses linked to credit cards that bought batteries in the last few weeks and Dan spent all day investigating them.

The one from my shop led him to a large house in the country about twenty miles away, and he's sure this is Vercetti's hideout. It's surrounded by iron railings and CCTV cameras and when he pulled up outside a man wearing a leather jacket and dark glasses strode down the drive.

He's going back with Doctor Infinity and Pi tomorrow to hack the phone calls and CCTV footage from the house. Mr and Mrs Amazing offered to spy on the house while picnicking in the one of the surrounding fields, but Dan refused. He said they'd blow years of hard work if they raised Vercetti's suspicions and made him flee.

We're closing in on the town's head of organized crime, not enjoying a pleasant day out. Sometimes I wonder if Mr and Mrs Amazing understand what a serious business they're mixed up in.

SATURDAY 12TH MARCH

Dan is now convinced the house belongs to Vercetti. Doctor Infinity and Pi piggybacked onto its phone and CCTV yesterday and identified Vercetti as a small man with a large nose and short black hair. There are two other figures living in the compound with him. One is bald with a scar on his left cheek and the other is tall with cropped blonde hair. Dan reckons these are Vercetti's bodyguards.

Dan wants to storm the house, overpower Vercetti

and leave him outside a police station along with all the evidence he's gathered against him.

We're going to strike late on Monday night, which doesn't give us long to prepare.

I can't believe we're on the cusp of capturing this town's crime boss. We'll be superhero legends after this.

East Dudchester League of Costumed Vigilantes (incorporating The Central Region Masked Crime-Fighters Society) assemble!

SUNDAY 13TH MARCH

Dan took us through his plan in a special meeting tonight.

'We'll arrive at 2330 hours,' he said. He emptied out a bag full of small black handguns. 'We'll run up to the gates carrying these.'

'In that case you can count me out,' said Mr Amazing. 'I hate criminal kingpins as much as the next man, but I don't want to be part of any missions that involve firearms.'

Dan picked up one of the guns, stuck it in his mouth and pulled the trigger. He took it out again and grinned.

'They're replicas,' he said. 'But Vercetti won't know and we might need to be very persuasive if he doesn't want to come.'

He pulled out a much bigger gun with a wide barrel. 'This is real, though. It will fire an electromagnetic pulse and take out all the electrics in the compound. The CCTV cameras will black out, the gate and doors will open and the phones will go down. If we're lucky, we'll get in and grab Vercetti before his guards find us. If not, it's going to get messy.'

Doctor Infinity took out a model of Vercetti's

compound and Dan stuck some plastic soldiers into position around it. 'Mr Amazing will drive the van, Pi will fire the pulse gun, and Doctor Infinity and I will take care of Vercetti. The Loner, Mrs Amazing and Amazagirl stand by the front gate in case we need your help with the guards. There are two of them and six of us so we have the advantage.'

'I can't do Mondays,' said Amazagirl, looking down at her phone.

'Fine,' said Dan, curling his hands so tightly that his knuckles went white. 'Then it will be five against two instead. Thanks for your help.'

UPDATE

I've been doing push-ups in my bedroom tonight to get in shape for fighting the guards tomorrow. I can do ten without needing a rest, so I should have a good chance if things turn nasty.

It's times like this I wish I'd spent my early years training with a secret martial arts group halfway up a mountain like Ratman did. But my parents would never have agreed to that. They wouldn't even let me go on the Tower of Terror when we went to Disneyland.

I can't believe Amazagirl has weaseled out of

superhero duty again. This is her chance to be part of the greatest crime-fighting mission this town has ever known and she isn't interested. I really don't understand some people.

MONDAY 14TH MARCH

Henry pestered me again at lunchtime. He kept asking when my league would be back in action soon and I got so sick of it I told him about the raid tonight. It was a massive relief to talk to someone about it after obsessing over it so much.

Every time I said something about our mission, he felt the need to invent nonsense about how his league are going to foil international smuggling rings, corrupt government agencies and cybercriminals.

I suppose my genuine plans are starting to sound like one of Henry's fantasies now. All that stuff about replica guns and electromagnetic devices sounds like I'm also copying things from an issue of *Ratman* or *Steel Guy*. If anyone had listened in to our conversation, they'd think we were both making it up.

It's just gone 10 p.m. now and I'm waiting for Mum and Dad to start snoring so I can cycle over to Dan's house. Let battle commence!

TUESDAY 15TH MARCH

It's now 4 a.m. and I'm back in my room. It all went wrong tonight and I don't know what to do. I can't talk to my parents, because they'll panic and call the police. And I can't talk to anyone else from the League, because they've all been captured by Vercetti.

We arrived outside the compound at 11:30 as planned. Pi fired his pulse gun at the gate and pushed it open. He crept down the gravel path, stopped a few metres

in front of the house and fired again. All the lights inside cut out.

Dan and Doctor Infinity crept down the dark pathway and went in. I stared at the murky windows, anxiously looking for some sign of them, but I couldn't make anything out.

After a few minutes I heard a door slam and saw movement outside the house. I was desperately hoping it would be Dan and Doctor Infinity dragging Vercetti up the path, but instead I made out the shape of three men running towards us.

The first figure to emerge from the gloom was Pi. He was dashing up the path with two guards chasing him. It looked like I was going to have to fight the guards after all. I was glad I'd done all those press-ups.

'They knew we were coming!' shouted Pi. 'Someone tipped them off!'

One of the men drew level with him, slammed his hand on Pi's shoulder and dragged him back down the path.

'Get out of here!' shouted Pi. 'Mission aborted!'

I rushed back to the van and Mrs Amazing followed. Mr Amazing was waiting in the front seat.

'We need to go, dear,' said Mrs Amazing. 'There's been a spot of bother.'

'That's a shame,' said Mr Amazing, turning his key in the ignition. 'What happened?'

The van chugged away down the lane. I glanced out the back window and saw one of Vercetti's guards rushing out of the gate.

'Hurry up!' I shouted.

'Turns out one of us is a rat,' said Mrs Amazing. She looked at me. 'We know it isn't us, so it must be The Loser.'

'The Loner,' I said. 'But it isn't me.'

Mr Amazing opened the glove compartment and peered inside. 'There's a spanner in here if you need to knock him out, dear.'

'No thanks, darling,' said Mrs Amazing. 'I'll just whack him with my replica gun if needs be.'

'Righty-oh,' said Mr Amazing. He stopped at the junction with the main road, looked both ways, then turned left.

'Hang on a minute,' I said. 'I'm not working for anyone. I just want to fight crime.'

'So who betrayed us?' asked Mr Amazing. 'It couldn't have been the others as they've all been captured.'

'Not all of them,' I said. 'What about your daughter? She's always saying crime-fighting is pointless and I notice she isn't here tonight. Maybe she tipped them off.'

'Don't be ridiculous,' shouted Mrs Amazing. 'As if Amy ... I mean, Amazagirl wouldn't put her own parents in danger.'

I thought it sounded like exactly the sort of thing she'd do, but I didn't push it any further.

There was no point in arguing, so I turned and stared out of the window as we drove on. I kept expecting to see Vercetti's guards speed up next to us, but nothing emerged.

It struck me that with Dan out of action, I was now official League leader, which wasn't going to go down well with Mr Amazing. But he was going to have to accept it so we could work together and solve the crisis.

When we arrived back in Dan's garage, Mr Amazing got out and held the door to the basement open for his wife. Instead of holding it open for me too, he let it slam in my face.

I was about to open it again when I heard screaming from inside the basement.

'Get off me!' shouted Mrs Amazing.

'Let me go or I'll shoot!' shouted Mr Amazing.

'With a replica gun?' replied another voice. 'I don't think so.'

I found myself whimpering, but stifled it so no one could hear. The garage door was still open, so I crept out and untied the Lonercycle from the tree at the front of the house. I jumped on it and rode away as

fast as I could. At the end of the street I looked over my shoulder and saw a tall man wearing dark glasses snooping around.

Vercetti's men were here too, which proved Amazagirl had betrayed us. It had to be her. No one

else could possibly have known where Dan's secret base was and that we were using replica guns.

I'm back home now and sick with worry. What should I do?

UPDATE

It's 6 a.m. and I've decided to go and see Amazagirl. Or as I should say, Amy Gibson. For once, I was glad she never made any effort to keep her identity secret.

I'm convinced she's the traitor and I'm worried she'll try and attack. But I'm sure she'll see the error of her ways when she finds her parents have been kidnapped and are probably being tortured right now.

No doubt she'll realize how foolish her disloyalty was, beg for my forgiveness and agree to come on a rescue mission with me.

ANOTHER UPDATE

I've just returned from Amy's house and I've come to the conclusion that she isn't the traitor after all. I've realized that the traitor was ... er ... me.

Amy's eyes looked really red when she opened the

door. She'd clearly had a sleepless night too. She started crying when I told her that her parents had been kidnapped, but insisted she hadn't contacted Vercetti's men.

'I haven't spoken a word to anyone about the League,' she said. 'I think it's a really stupid hobby, but I would never put Mum and Dad in danger by tipping off criminals. You must have betrayed them. There's no one else who could have done it.'

'I'd never tell a criminal about our secret activities,' I said. 'I'd never tell anyone at all, in fact.'

I thought about this for a moment and a horrible thought struck me. There was someone I'd shared our secrets with. Someone who was really terrible at keeping them. Uh-oh.

I tried to run through what I'd told Henry. I'd mentioned we were planning a raid on the house. Had I mentioned we were using replica guns? Had I told him where Dan's base was? Sadly, I'd told him everything.

But how could Henry be a spy? Spies are meant to keep secrets, not run around shouting them at the top of their voices.

As if Henry could have met some genuine criminals

and, more importantly, resisted the urge to brag about it. It's hard enough to shut him up about his imaginary friends.

Maybe he's really a calm, level-headed boy with a firm grasp on reality. I don't know what to believe any more.

I'm going to wait outside the school and confront him as soon as he turns up. I haven't been this angry with him since he filled in the crossword in my *Ratman* annual.

ANOTHER UPDATE

Henry looked genuinely confused when I accused him of being a spy. For a moment I wondered if I was really on the right track after all. Then I remembered his rival superhero league.

'Could you describe the other members to me?' I asked.

'Of course,' said Henry. 'There's Captain Laser, who can fire lasers out of his eyes, Timewave, who can pause time, Terry Kinesis, who can move objects with his mind...'

'And you've seen them do this, have you?'

'No,' said Henry. 'But they told me about it.'

'What did they actually look like when you saw them?' I asked.

'Terry Kinesis is small with a large nose and black hair,' said Henry. 'Captain Laser is bald with a scar down his cheek. And Timewave is tall with blond hair.'

It didn't take me long to work out what had happened.

When Vercetti began to get reports about costumed vigilantes meddling with his crimes, he sent his henchmen to look for them. All they managed to find was Henry, leaping around the cinema car park in his Ninja Kid costume, and brought him back to their boss.

It soon became obvious to Vercetti that Henry was not a sophisticated vigilante, but an excitable boy without much grip on reality. Yet he had a link with the genuine vigilantes through me, so Vercetti strung him along with the notion of a rival crime-fighting league.

Henry passed on all the information I leaked to him, which just goes to show you can't be too careful what you say, even in school grounds.

The whole incident with the ATM bomb was designed to lure us into the trap at Vercetti's hideout. His technical advisor even programmed the clock to stop at 3.14 seconds as a joke at Pi's expense.

I feel bad I leaked the information and Henry feels

bad about passing it on to a bunch of criminals he thought were his friends. We've both let everyone down and need to find a way to make amends.

ANOTHER UPDATE

As temporary leader of the League, I need to work out what to do. I can't return to our base, because it's been infiltrated by the enemy. And I'm way past the point where I can get the police involved. Perhaps if they'd gone for the searchlight plan a couple of months ago we'd be working side by side now, but they made their decision.

What would Ratman do?

In issue 323, Crossword Clue breaks Ratman's back and throws him into a prison at the bottom of a well that no one has ever escaped from. But even in these desperate circumstances, he doesn't give up. He fixes his back by making a sling out of a bed sheet and constructs a brand new Ratcopter using the metal frame of his bed.

Ratman made the best of his poor resources and I've got to do the same. I'm going to reform the League using the only superheroes I have left. Sadly, that means I'm going to have to ask Henry to join.

ANOTHER UPDATE

I called Amy at lunch and told her I'm forming a new version of the League with an additional member and that we needed to meet at her house. She asked if this new member was a complete idiot. I didn't want her to feel negative about our chances of rescuing the others, so I said he wasn't. She's not going to be pleased when she finds out.

Henry was overjoyed about joining. He ran around the playing field shouting, 'Ninja Kid revenge' and it took me ages to calm him down. I said he couldn't join unless he proved he could be serious, so he put on a solemn expression. But I could tell he was still really excited, because he spent all afternoon drawing pictures of The Ninja Kid beating up criminals.

ANOTHER UPDATE

This evening we had the first meeting of the League Mark II. We gathered in Amy's front room, which was full of the porcelain animal figurines her parents collect. It took ages to get Henry to stop playing with them and tell us everything he could remember about Vercetti's hideout.

He says that Vercetti spends most of his time in his office, which is at the back of the house and contains a bank of CCTV screens. His bodyguards hang out in the room to the left of the front door. There are several empty rooms upstairs, and he reckons this is where they'll be holding the prisoners.

Henry's been trying to get Vercetti to hold another meeting of their supposed league for ages, but he keeps saying he's too busy.

If Henry turns up at Vercetti's house, demands a meeting, and shares his brilliant idea about what their league should do next, they will have no choice but to let him in and talk him out of it. This will draw Vercetti's guards into the office and leave the front of the house unguarded. He'll position himself in front of the CCTV screens and deliver his ridiculous new vision for the league.

While he's doing this, we'll sneak into the house, go upstairs and set everyone free.

I think this is a good plan because it lets everyone play to their strengths: in my case, being an amazing superhero; in Henry's case, spouting nonsense.

There's no time to lose, so we're going to cycle down to Vercetti's house tonight.

IN CASE I AM DEAD

I am just about to set off on a very dangerous rescue mission and am writing this in case I die and my secret diary is discovered.

As you can tell, I lost my life in the fight against crime. I tried to make the world a better place and I regret nothing. Unless I died because of something stupid Henry did, in which case I regret inviting him.

Please respect my final wishes:
DO NOT throw away my comic collection. It's highly valuable and deserves to end up in the hands of a serious collector. Please sell it to a proper comic shop and use the proceeds to build a statue of The Loner in the town centre.

If someone wants to assume the mantel of The Loner after I'm gone, I'm fine with that. I'm well aware that Jennings Melman took over as Ratman after Crossword Clue killed Chip Browning in issue 432. Just

make sure they're doing it because they really hate crime rather than for the glory.

If Henry is still alive, he must read out the following statements at my funeral:

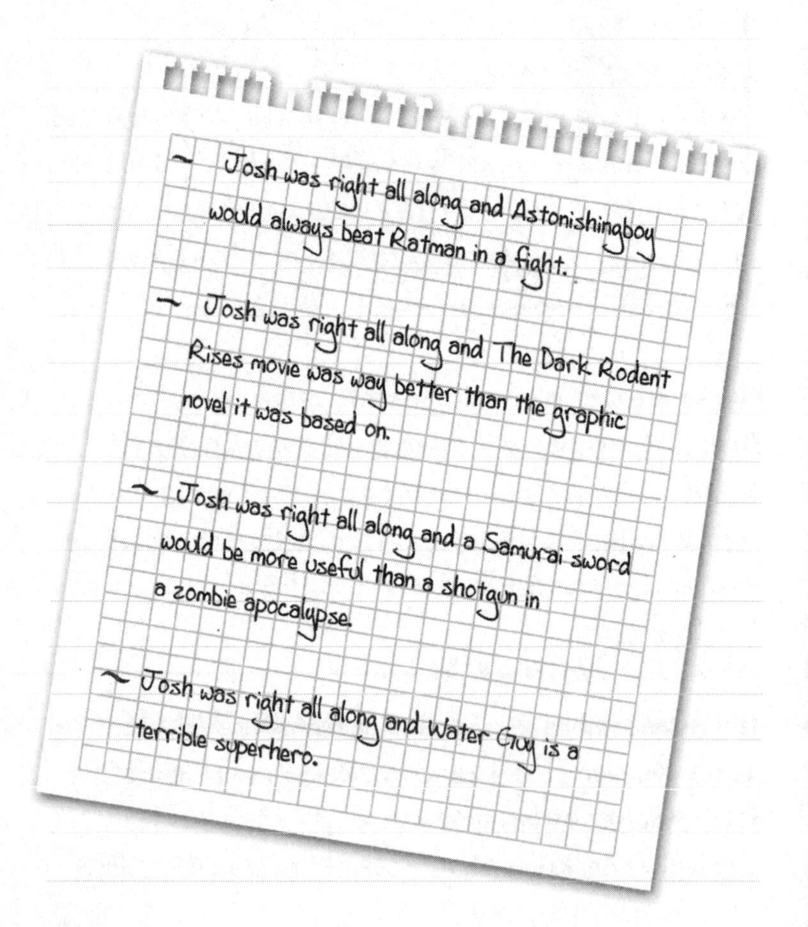

If a film version of my life is to be made, a serious director like Crispin Canterbury must be behind it. I want to be shown as a moody and serious character played by an award-winning actor, not an annoying skateboarder with a talking dog sidekick.

WEDNESDAY 16TH MARCH

Henry insisted on wearing his underpants over his costume on our rescue mission, as he said it made him feel more like Astonishingboy.

Not that Astonishingboy actually wears underpants

over his suit, of course. He has red shorts integrated into his costume because he was modelled on a circus strongman. And even if he did wear underpants on top of his costume, he wouldn't choose baggy boxer shorts with holes in the back like Henry did.

It took us ages to cycle to Vercetti's house. I'd forgotten how far it was because I've only been by car before. We were all so tired by the time we arrived we had to stop at the end of the lane for a while to get our energy back. Even Henry was too tired to run around, so he lay on the grass and shouted, 'Ninja Kid revenge'.

We tied our bikes to a streetlight and made our way down the lane. Amazagirl and I crouched behind a wall while Henry strode ahead and buzzed the intercom.

'Hello?' asked a deep voice.

'It's me,' said Henry. 'The Ninja Kid. I've come for a meeting of the League of Awesome Crusaders.'

'We're busy,' said the voice. 'Go home and we'll call you.'

'I need to see Terry Kinesis,' said Henry. 'I've had an idea about what the League should be doing and I think he'll want to hear about it.'

'He's not in,' said the voice.

'My idea is that we should work more closely with the police,' said Henry. 'Isn't that fabulous? I'll invite them round here for a meeting so we can discuss the best ways to fight crime together.'

There was an angry murmur on the other end of the intercom, then a short buzz and the gate swung open.

Henry wandered in. I rushed forward and shoved a rock into the gap so it wouldn't close fully.

We waited for a couple of minutes and crept up to the gate. Amazagirl squeezed herself through the gap and I followed. When I was halfway through, I felt a tugging around my neck. I turned to see that my cape had impaled itself on one of the spikes. I tried to untangle it, but it was held fast.

'Get rid of it!' hissed Amazagirl.

I ripped open the Velcro attachment and followed her down the drive. I felt much less like a superhero

without my cape flapping behind me, but I suppose it was more practical.

I sometimes wonder why so many superheroes still bother with capes. Over the years, Ratman's cape has been snagged on cars, trains and the giant hands of skyscraper clocks. He'll never be stuck for a picnic blanket, but it's a high price to pay.

We sneaked up to the front door and pushed it open. Inside was a wide hallway with a flight of stairs to the right. The walls and carpet were red, the

bannisters were gold and there were marble statues of cherubs on plinths and in niches. It seemed a shame that someone had bothered to amass so much wealth just to spend it on horrible stuff.

We sneaked upstairs, treading softly on the thick carpet. There was a landing halfway up the stairs with a stuffed hyena on. Where did Vercetti even buy this stuff? Is there a chain of tacky furniture shops for rich criminals?

From the back office, I could hear Henry saying, 'I've designed a special light we can shine in the sky to contact the police commissioner.'

'I don't think that's a good idea,' Vercetti was saying. 'And I'm really busy right now.'

Upstairs was another long corridor with six doors. I tried one on the left. Inside was a room that smelled of aftershave with mirrored ceilings, a four-poster bed and some discarded leopard-print underpants.

I tried a door on the right. Inside was a jacuzzi shaped like a shell surrounded by gold drapes and champagne flutes.

It made me angry that Vercetti would steal money from innocent citizens to fund his dreadful taste, and that only sharpened my resolve to bring him to justice.

'Over here,' whispered Amazagirl. She rushed into a room at the far end of the corridor and I followed.

Dan, Pi, Doctor Infinity, Mr Amazing and Mrs Amazing were tied to chairs in the middle of the room. Their arms were bound with thick rope and they had strips of duct tape covering their mouths.

Amazagirl pressed her finger to her lips and circled round them before starting to untie her mum's ropes. I dashed round to the other end of the chairs and tried untying Dan's ropes, but it was really difficult.

Amazagirl worked her way down the line really quickly, shoved me out the way and undid Dan's ropes too. Then she went back and whipped the duct tape away from their mouths one by one. I stared at the others with my finger pressed to my lips as she did so. They mouthed cries of pain and wiped tears from their eyes, but none of them made a sound.

Mr Amazing looked like he was about to say something, but Amazagirl shook her head. Quite right, too. This wasn't the time for him to start moaning about the standards of hospitality during his kidnapping.

I stepped out into the hallway and the others

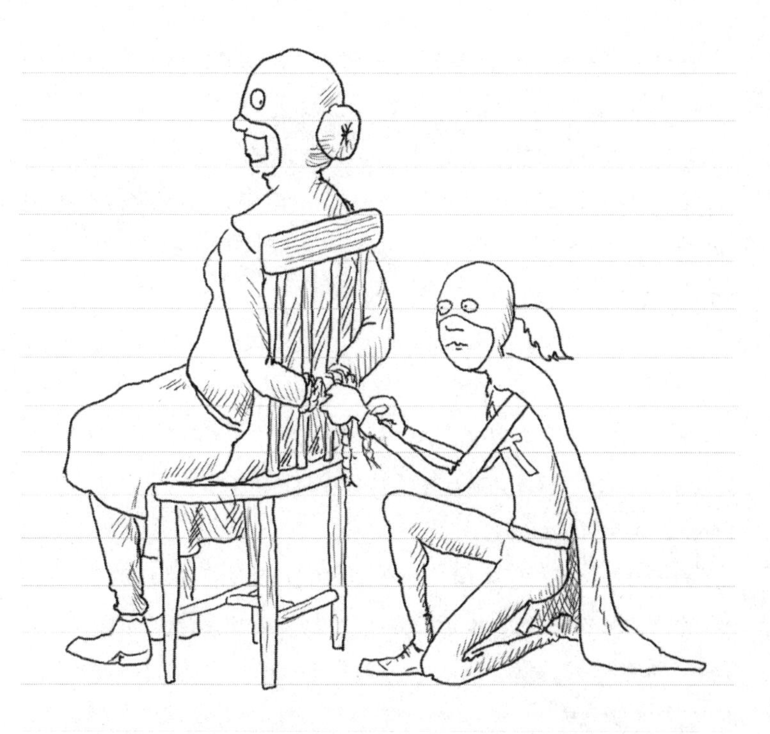

followed. I nearly knocked over the stuffed hyena on the way downstairs, but Dan rushed forward and caught it.

We were almost at the bottom when Henry rushed out of Vercetti's office. He was wincing slightly.

'I think I might have moved away from the screens,' he said. 'And they might have seen you.'

Vercetti's guards stepped out of the office behind him.

Henry let out a cry of terror and dashed out the front door. This wasn't a great first impression to make on the rest of the League. He'd messed up the plan, yelped in fright and run away. I know Dan likes to invite everyone into the League, but I was sure he'd make an exception after that pathetic display.

The bodyguards scowled at us.

I tried shouting, 'East Dudchester League of Costumed Vigilantes (incorporating The Central Region Masked Crime-Fighters Society) assemble!' but the guards charged at us before I'd even got to the brackets.

Dan, Amazagirl, Doctor Infinity and Pi shoved past me to take them on. Mr and Mrs Amazing ran back upstairs.

I stood on the stairs, uncertain about what to do. Obviously, as a brilliant hero, it was my duty to charge forward and join in the fight. On the other hand, if I ran away and hid I wouldn't be the only one.

Dan hit the blonde guard in the face and there was a faint snapping noise, as if someone had stepped on a twig. Blood gushed out of his nose and sprayed over the front of his shirt. He'd need to get that in the wash as soon as the fight was over, or it would stain.

The guard reacted quickly, though, and punched Dan on the cheek, who staggered sideways, grunting with pain. I'd seen fights in school, but they were nothing like this. They usually consisted of two boys pushing each other in the middle of a crowd until a teacher broke it up. Real fights weren't nearly as much fun to watch.

Doctor Infinity, Amazagirl and Pi grabbed the bald guard. Between them they managed to wrestle him back and tip his head up.

'Come on, Loser!' shouted Amazagirl. 'Help us!'

I strode down the stairs, clenching my fingers. I'd never have such a clean shot on a villain again. All I had to do was draw my fist back, fling it forward and dispense some justice.

'I'm not The Loser,' I said. 'I'm The Loner.'

I threw my fist at the guard's chin.

It wasn't what I was expecting. For a start, I didn't think it would hurt my hand so much. It was like slamming my fist into a wall covered in stubble. Also, isn't punching someone meant to hurt them at least a bit? This guy just laughed as I cradled my sore fist.

Mr and Mrs Amazing came rushing back down the stairs, holding the ropes they'd been tied to the chairs with. So they hadn't been running from the danger after all. I was glad I hadn't followed.

They fastened the ropes around the hands of the bald guard.

Dan thumped the blonde guard to the floor and wrestled him into a headlock.

'Tie his legs!' he shouted. 'Neutralize the threat!'

I pushed past the mass of squirming superheroes and guards. Someone needed to take on the real villain.

I rushed to the end of the hallway and kicked open the door to Vercetti's office. It slammed shut again, because I'd kicked it too hard. I opened it by the handle instead and stepped inside.

There he was. The mastermind behind all the crime in our town.

Vercetti was sitting behind a wide wooden desk at the far end of the room, leaning back in his chair and grinning.

On CCTV screens to my right, I could see the rest of the League still struggling with the guards.

'The Loner's here,' I said. 'And it looks like you'll be spending some long lonely years in prison.'

I had absolutely no idea what to do next. I didn't want to hit him, as my hand was still sore from punching the guard and I couldn't think of any more one-liners. In desperation, I looked down at my utility belt. I unhooked my tape measure and threw it at

Vercetti. It flew wide and bounced off a horrible lamp that was meant to look like a goddess holding a torch.

I let off all my remaining Lonersnaps and stink bombs one by one. I knew I should be using them as a distraction to launch an awesome attack, but I couldn't bring myself to attempt one. I'd just found out that punching someone in the face was harder than I expected, so back-flipping over a desk and launching into a mid-air judo move didn't seem like a great idea.

Vercetti reached into his desk drawer and pulled out a handgun. I couldn't believe he was going straight from stink bomb to gun. He could have escalated things gradually with a firecracker or smoke bomb.

'And it looks like you'll be spending some long lonely years underground,' said Vercetti, standing up and pointing the gun at me.

I didn't think his retort worked very well, because it implied I'd emerge from my grave one day as a zombie or something. I tried to explain this, but all that came out was, 'Please don't kill me.'

I heard feet stomping into the room behind me. I breathed a sigh of relief. Dan must have overpowered the guards and come to rescue me. But when I turned

round, I saw it was Henry who'd entered. Now I was certain I was going to die.

'Ninja Kid to the rescue,' shouted Henry. He leapt around the room, flinging his arms around.

'Stop it, Henry!' I shouted. 'This is serious! He's got a real gun!'

Henry took no notice. He just kept flailing around and shouting 'Ninja Kid and The Loser are in the house!' I hadn't seen him this excited since he got hold of the limited variant cover edition of *Ratman* issue 831.

'Stop that or I'll shoot,' said Vercetti.

'I don't believe anything you say anymore,' said Henry. 'You told me you could move objects with your mind, you massive liar.'

I heard a loud bang and flinched. It took me a few seconds to realize this was what gunfire sounded like in real life.

I opened my eyes and saw Henry looking down and patting his costume. The bullet had completely missed him. He fixed Vercetti with a mean stare. It was the same look he'd given Mr Singh that time he'd tried to confiscate his musical *Ratman* keyring.

'That was your last warning,' said Vercetti. He aimed his gun at Henry's head.

'Ninja attack!' shouted Henry. He rushed forward and launched himself into the air. He flew over the desk and slammed into Vercetti with both feet.

Vercetti's head cracked into the wall behind him

and he slumped to the floor. His gun went spinning across the carpet.

Henry landed next to Vercetti, got to his feet and shouted, 'Ninja power!'

Dan rushed in, followed by the others. He scooped up Vercetti's arms and bound them behind his back with rope. Vercetti opened his eyes and struggled weakly against him.

Mr Amazing was about to pick up the gun when Dan shouted, 'Leave it for the police. We need his prints on it.'

When Vercetti was fully bound and gagged, Dan dumped him in the hallway next to the guards, who were also tied securely with rope and duct tape.

We strolled out of the house and down the drive. I untangled my cape from the front gate, but it had a huge rip down the back. There was no point in trying to wear it now, so I scrunched it into a ball and carried it.

When we got back to the bikes, a serious flaw in our plan became apparent. We had seven superheroes and just three bikes. Even if we could cram two vigilantes onto each bike, someone would still have to walk the twenty miles home. And after kidnappings, sleepless

nights and criminal-bashing, you're in the mood for a deep bath rather than a long hike.

Mr Amazing suggested that we look for a night bus, but nobody liked the idea. Amazagirl said that she'd taken one before and even though we were dressed as superheroes and covered in blood and sweat, we still wouldn't be the weirdest people on it.

In the end, Dan agreed to ride Amazagirl's bike back to his house and return for the rest of us in the van.

I doubt we looked very dignified as we hung around the side of a country road in our costumes. We got a few jeers

from passing cars, but I was so pleased about defeating the town's worst ever criminal I took no notice.

I didn't get back home until after 3 a.m., but I still managed to force myself out of bed and got to school on time. Now we've wiped out all the crime in the town I might not need to be a superhero anymore, so I'd better pay more attention in lessons.

THURSDAY 17TH MARCH

Vercetti was arrested yesterday. According to the news, police raided his house and seized millions in stolen goods and illegal firearms. There was no mention of superheroes, thankfully.

Henry pestered me about the League all day in school, so I've agreed to bring him along tomorrow. I only really invited him to join the League Mark II, and now the original version is back, he'll have to reapply to Dan for membership. But I could hardly refuse after he saved my life.

I'm starting to think Henry could make a pretty good superhero if he learned to concentrate. I saw a steely, determined side to him yesterday that I usually only see when he's trying to get out of playing sports. If he can focus his energy on fighting crime

and avoid getting carried away, he could be a good asset in the fight against evil.

I really hope he learns to keep his mouth shut, though. I know I shouldn't have told him all those secrets in the first place, but passing them on to an obvious criminal gang was really silly.

I tried to teach him how to brood at lunchtime so he could become a more serious crime-fighter. We sneaked out onto the science block roof and I told him to look out across the town and consider our responsibilities to the public. He managed it for two minutes before jumping around and shouting 'Ninja attack!' He almost fell off and ignored me when I told him to come back and keep still.

Mr Singh heard the noise from the classroom below and didn't believe me when I said we were retrieving a football. We both got detention for climbing onto the roof, even though Henry was the only one being irresponsible.

FRIDAY 18TH MARCH

I took Henry along to Dan's house half an hour before the meeting to see if he'd accept him into the League.

Dan made him shout 'I really hate crime' over and over again at the top of his voice, which wasn't a great idea. Henry was already overexcited about the idea of joining, and this wound him up to dangerous levels of giddiness.

He also let him have a glass of actual Coke, which didn't help. He's only allowed the caffeine-free stuff at home.

When the others arrived, we went down to the basement and Dan congratulated everyone on capturing Vercetti. He singled out Amazagirl and me as having shown initiative, and she couldn't stop herself from smiling briefly.

Mr Amazing said my rescue mission more than made

up for causing the whole mess by giving our secrets away, which was a backhanded compliment if ever I've heard one. I think he was trying to have me demoted from deputy leader, but Dan didn't rise to it.

Dan talked about the vacuum of power at the heart of the town's criminal community now Vercetti has been arrested. He ran us through some of the other criminals Vercetti has associated with and speculated about which ones might take over.

So it looks as though I spoke too soon when I said we'd wiped out all crime forever, but I don't mind if it means I can keep on being an awesome superhero.

Henry shouted 'I really hate crime' every time Dan said the name of a criminal and he was soon walking about and fidgeting.

He began to fiddle with Pi's remote control devices and I told him to sit down and concentrate, but he took no notice. I saw him pick up Pi's electromagnetic pulse gun, but it was too late to stop him.

He shouted, 'I really hate crime' and pressed the button on the gun, plunging the basement into darkness.

'Whoops,' said Henry. 'I didn't know it would do that.'

SATURDAY 19TH MARCH

I stayed behind to help Dan after the meeting yesterday. Pi and Doctor Infinity got the electrics running again and checked all their equipment, and I gave Dan a hand defrosting his freezer.

He lost quite a lot of food when it cut out, because he always prepares and freezes his meals after his weekly shop to make sure the government can't inject chemicals into them.

I apologized for bringing Henry, and Dan stuck to his line that it's always safer to include new costumed vigilantes in the League, no matter how idiotic they are. I bet he wasn't expecting one as silly as The Ninja Kid, though.

It made me glad that our part in the downfall of Vercetti was kept out of the news. If we ever get hyped in the media you can bet there will be a long queue of wannabe heroes turning up at Dan's door, some of whom will make Henry seem sensible.

SUNDAY 20TH MARCH

Henry came round with a gift today. To thank me for inviting him into the League, he got his mum to make me a replacement cape. And this time she's spelled

the word 'Loner' correctly on the back, so my costume is finally complete.

I tried to test out my new cape by climbing on top of our roof and letting it flap majestically in the wind. Unfortunately, the wind was so strong it blew over my head and I nearly fell off. I decided it would be safer to brood at ground level on windy days.

Not that I'm in much of a mood for brooding anyway. We've just beaten our local crime boss, and I'm convinced we can deal with whatever threats this town throws at us next. The East Dudchester League of Costumed Vigilantes (incorporating The Central Region Masked Crime-Fighters Society) have assembled, and crime doesn't stand a chance.

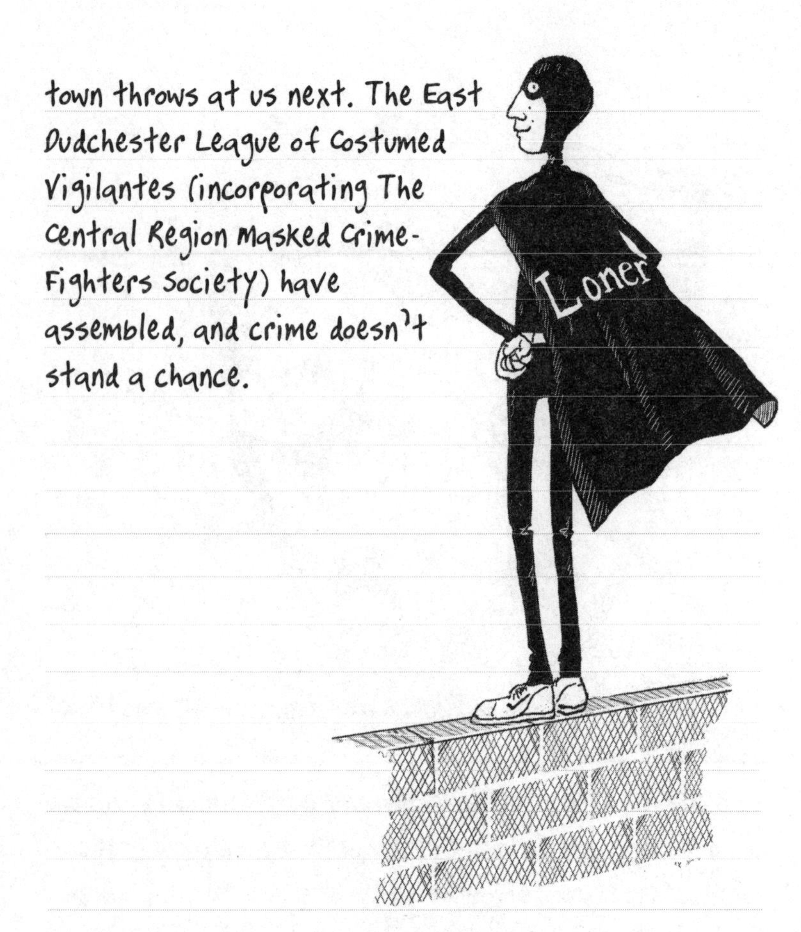

THE EAST DUDCHESTER
LEAGUE
OF
COSTUMED VIGILANTES
incorporating
THE CENTRAL REGION
MASKED CRIME-FIG
SOCIETY

ALSO BY TIM COLLINS

Diary of a Wimpy Vampire
978-1-84317-458-5
£7.99

Diary of a Wimpy Vampire: Prince of Dorkness
978-1-84317-524-7
£7.99

Adventures of a Wimpy Werewolf
978-1-84317-856-9
£7.99

The Wimpy Vampire Strikes Back
978-1-78243-022-3
£7.99